DC SUPER HERO GIRLS

FINALS CRISIS

an original graphic novel

WRITTEN BY **Shea Fontana**

ART BY **Yancey Labat**

COLORS BY **Monica Kubina**

LETTERING BY **Janice Chiang**

SUPERGIRL BASED ON THE CHARACTERS CREATED
BY JERRY SIEGEL AND JOE SHUSTER.
BY SPECIAL ARRANGEMENT WITH
THE JERRY SIEGEL FAMILY.

DC SUPER HERO GIRLS: FINALS CRISIS. July, 2016.
Published by DC Comics, 2900 W. Alameda Avenue, Burbank, CA 91505. GST # is R125921072.
Copyright © 2016 DC Comics. All Rights Reserved. All characters featured in this issue,
the distinctive likenesses thereof and related elements are trademarks of DC Comics.
The stories, characters and incidents mentioned in this magazine are entirely fictional.
DC Comics does not read or accept unsolicited submissions of ideas, stories or artwork.
This book is manufactured at a facility holding chain-of-custody certification. This paper is made
with sustainably managed North American fiber. For Advertising and Custom Publishing contact
dccomicsadvertising@dccomics.com. For details on DC Comics Ratings, visit dccomics.com/go/ratings.
Printed by Transcontinental Interglobe, Beauceville, QC, Canada. 5/6/16. ISBN: 978-1-4012-6247-1

PEFC

PEFC/01-31-10/

TABLE OF CONTENTS

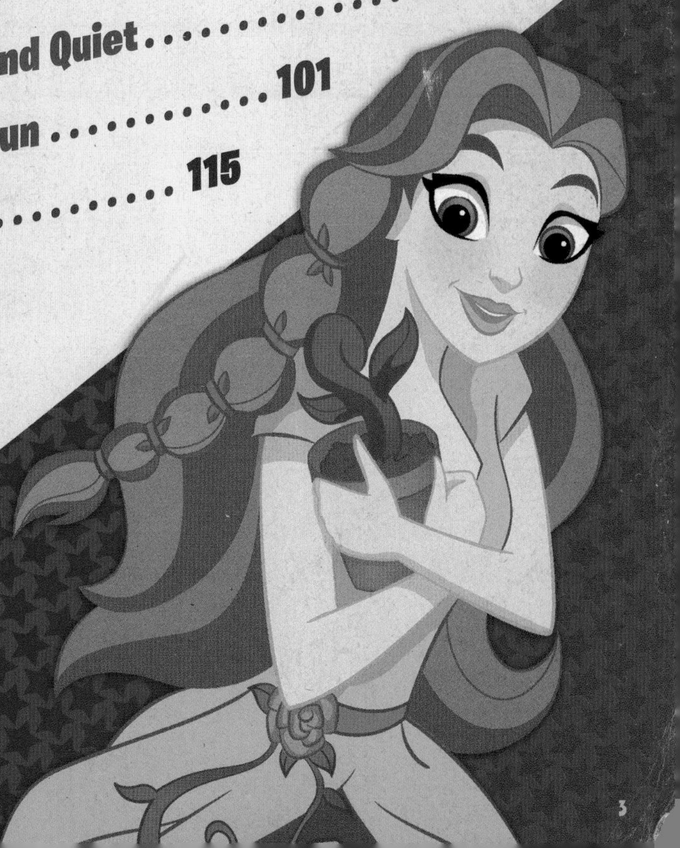

SUPER HERO HIGH SCHOOL

WONDER WOMAN

SUPER-POWERS
Super-strength, flight, near-invincibility, super-athleticism

SUPER HERO HIGH SCHOOL

SUPERGIRL

SUPER-POWERS
Super-strength, flight, invincibility, super-hearing, heat vision, x-ray vision

SUPER HERO HIGH SCHOOL

BATGIRL

SUPER-POWERS
Computer genius, expert martial artist, photographic memory, legendary detective skills

SUPER HERO HIGH SCHOOL

BUMBLEBEE

SUPER-POWERS
Enhanced strength, flight, ability to shrink, projects stinger blasts

SUPER HERO HIGH SCHOOL

POISON IVY

SUPER-POWERS
Genius-level intellect, summons and controls plants

CALL

HARLEY QUINN

SUPER HERO HIGH SCHOOL

SUPER-POWERS
Expert gymnast, acrobat, quick-witted class clown

KATANA

SUPER HERO HIGH SCHOOL

SUPER-POWERS
Champion Samurai sword fighter, expert martial artist, painter

BEAST BOY

SUPER HERO HIGH SCHOOL

SUPER-POWERS
Shape shifts into any animal form, world-class slacker

AMANDA WALLER

SUPER HERO HIGH SCHOOL

Principal

STAFF

GORILLA GRODD

SUPER HERO HIGH SCHOOL

Vice-principal

STAFF

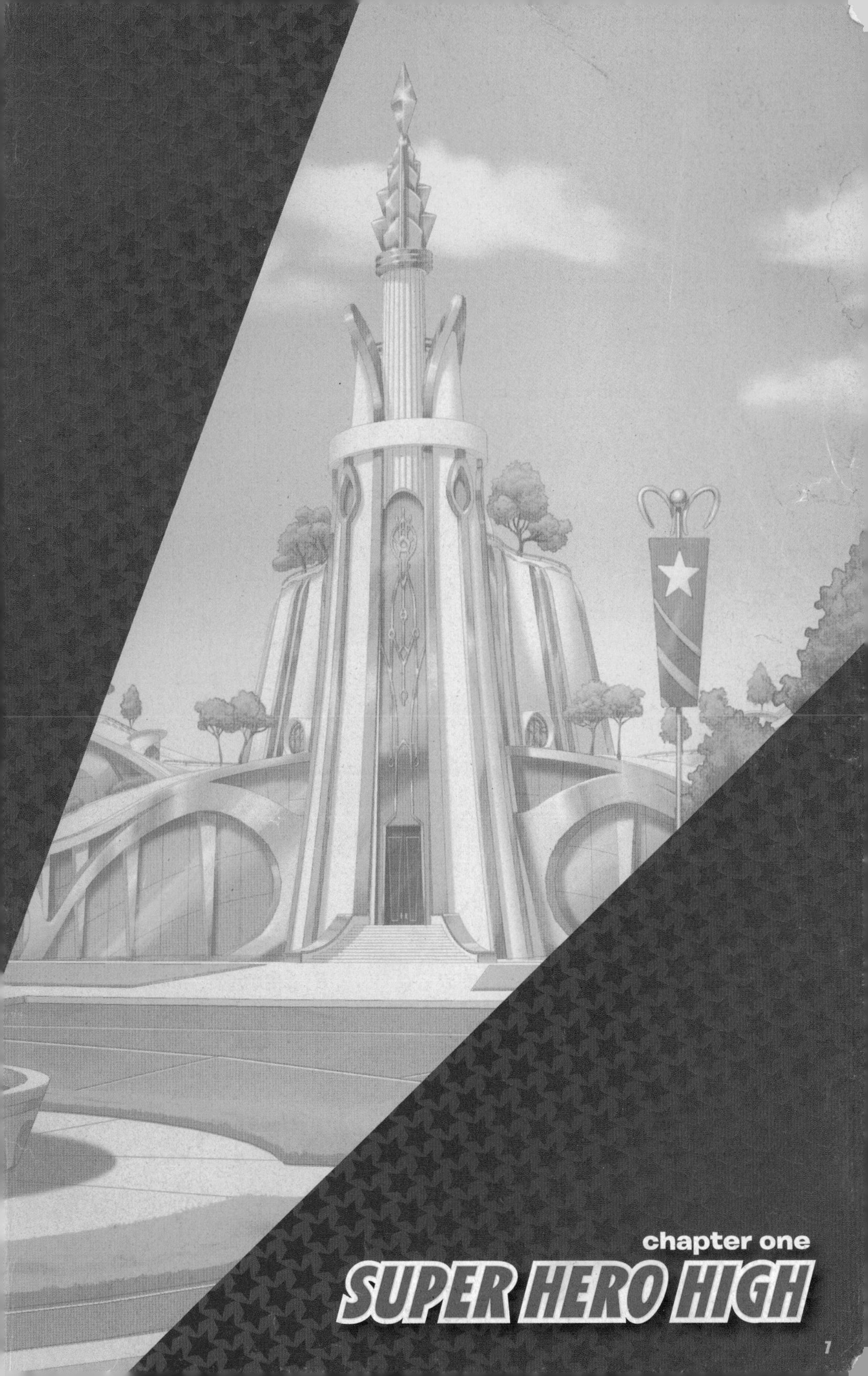

chapter one

SUPER HERO HIGH

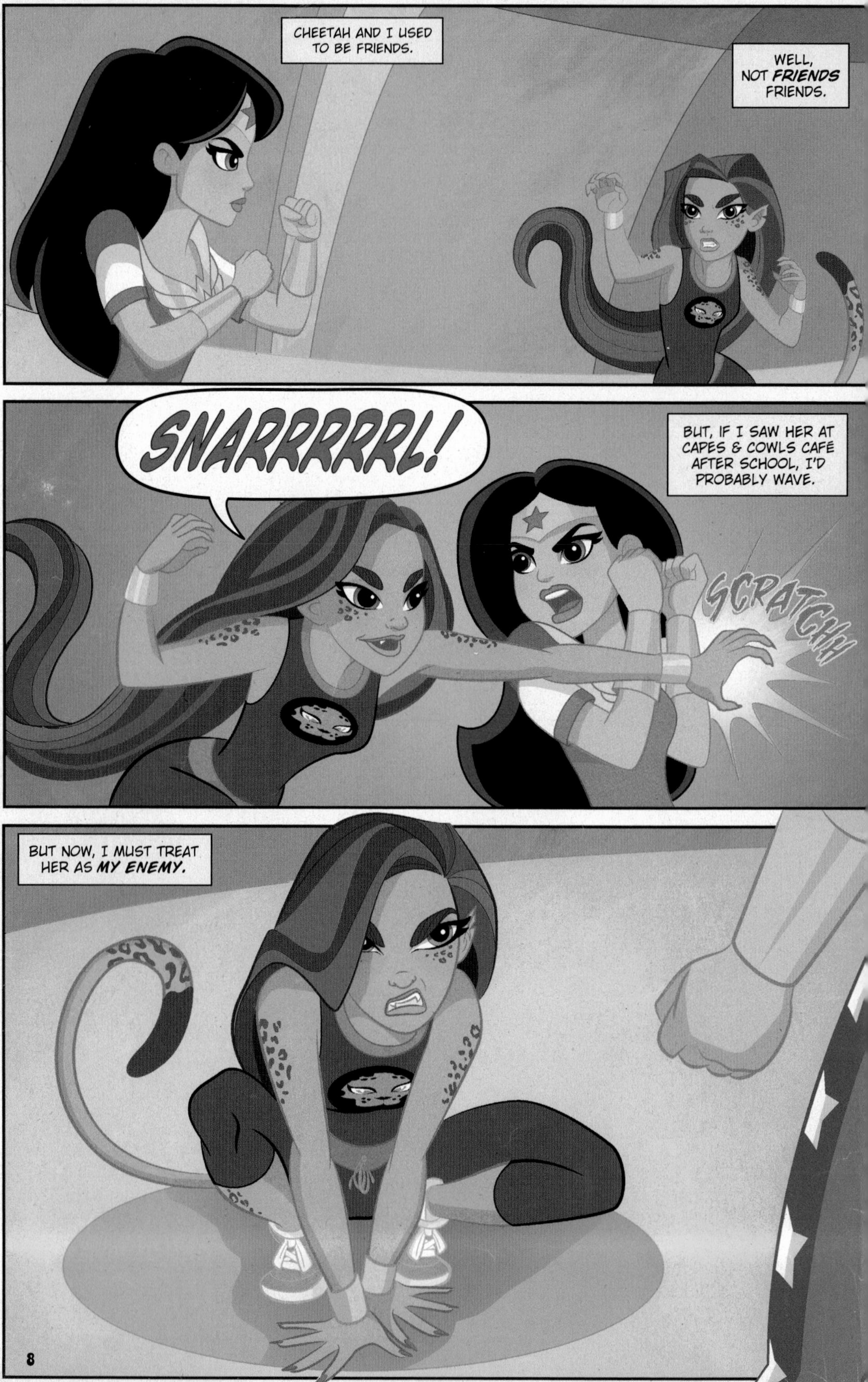
CHEETAH AND I USED TO BE FRIENDS.
WELL, NOT FRIENDS FRIENDS.
SNARRRRRRL!
BUT, IF I SAW HER AT CAPES & COWLS CAFÉ AFTER SCHOOL, I'D PROBABLY WAVE.
SCRATCHH
BUT NOW, I MUST TREAT HER AS MY ENEMY.

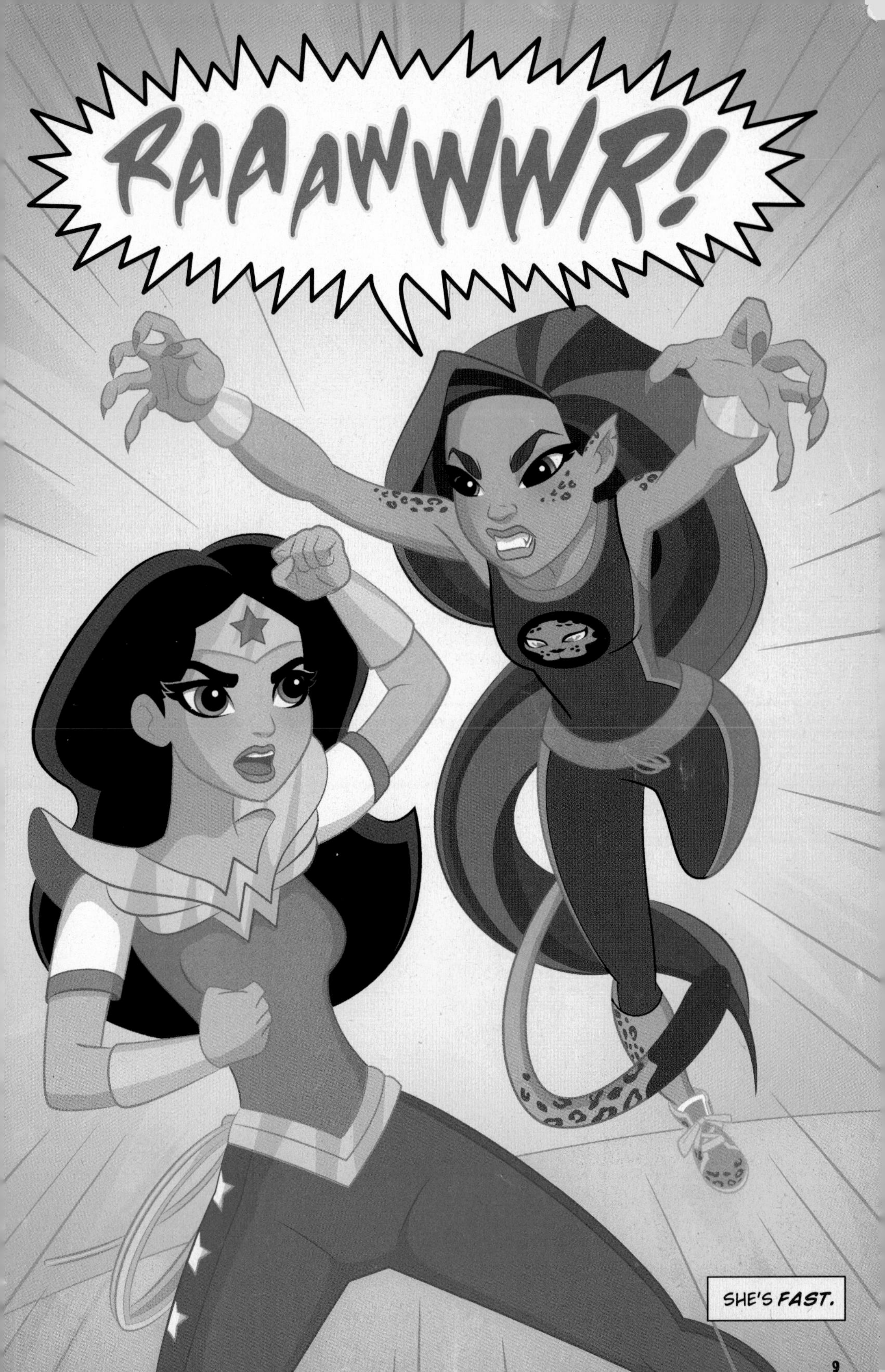
RAAAWWWR!
SHE'S FAST.

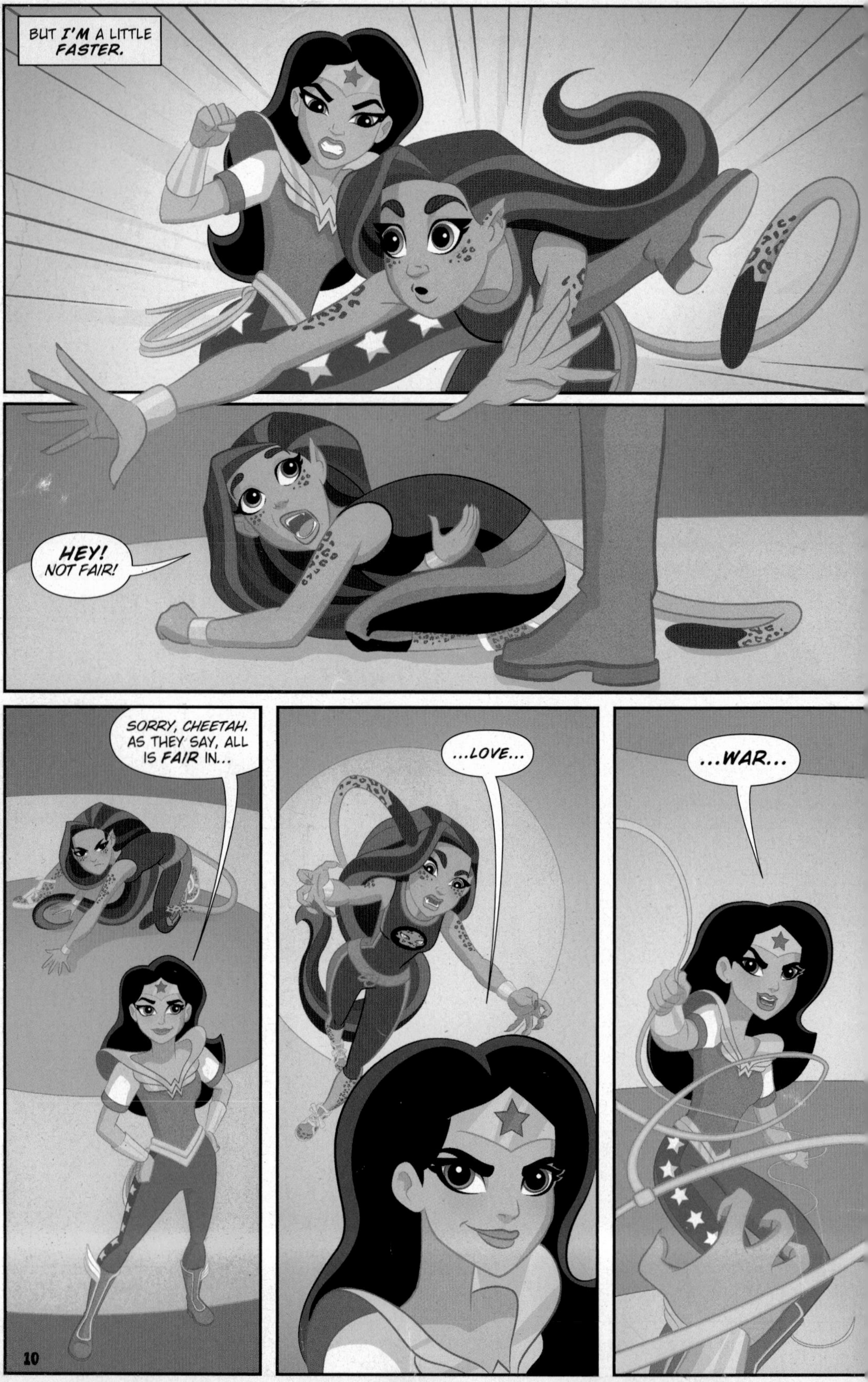
BUT I'M A LITTLE FASTER.
HEY! NOT FAIR!
SORRY, CHEETAH. AS THEY SAY, ALL IS FAIR IN...
...LOVE...
...WAR...

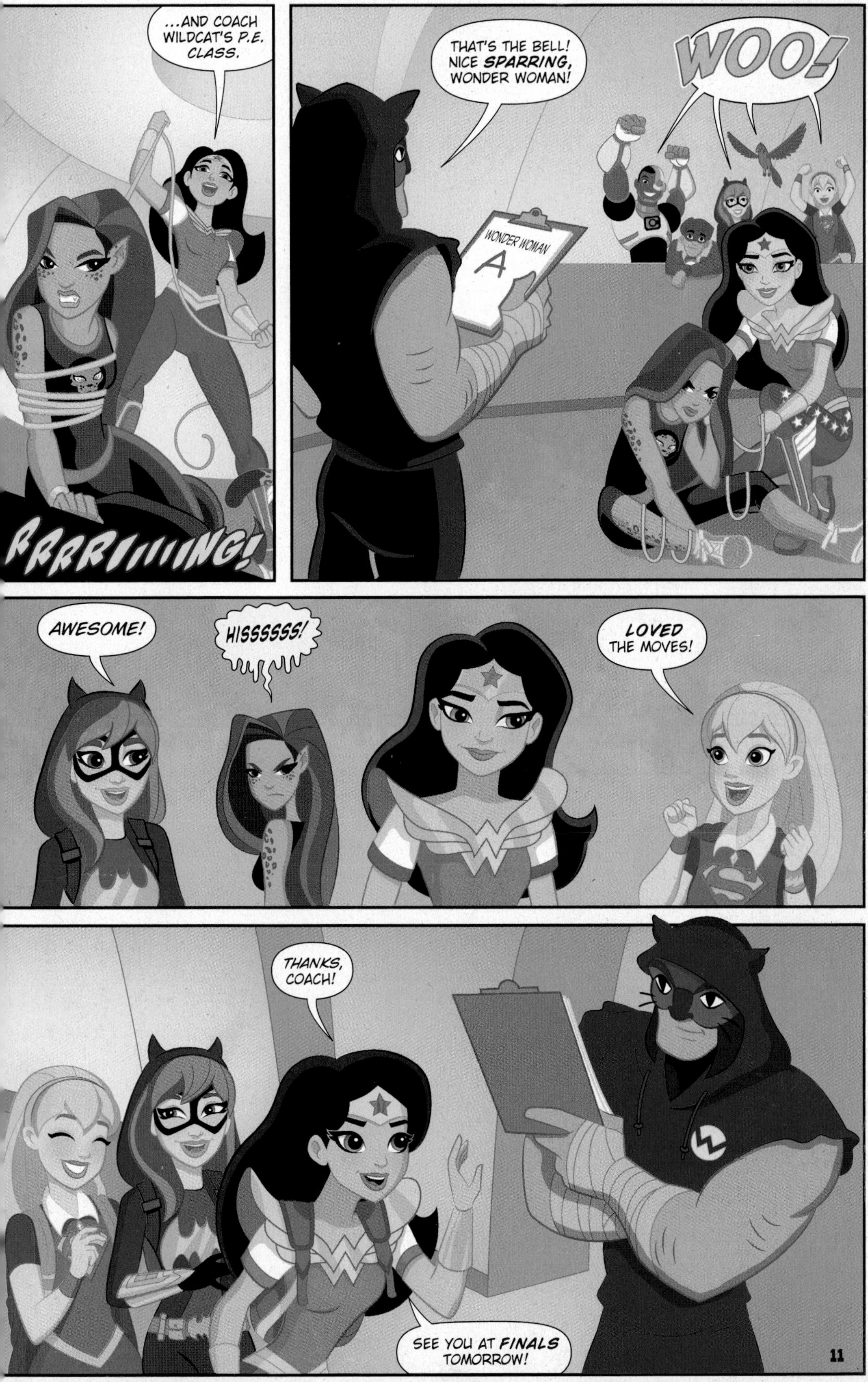
...AND COACH WILDCAT'S P.E. CLASS.
RRRRIIIIIING!
THAT'S THE BELL! NICE SPARRING, WONDER WOMAN!
WONDER WOMAN
A
WOO!
AWESOME!
HISSSSSS!
LOVED THE MOVES!
THANKS, COACH!
SEE YOU AT FINALS TOMORROW!

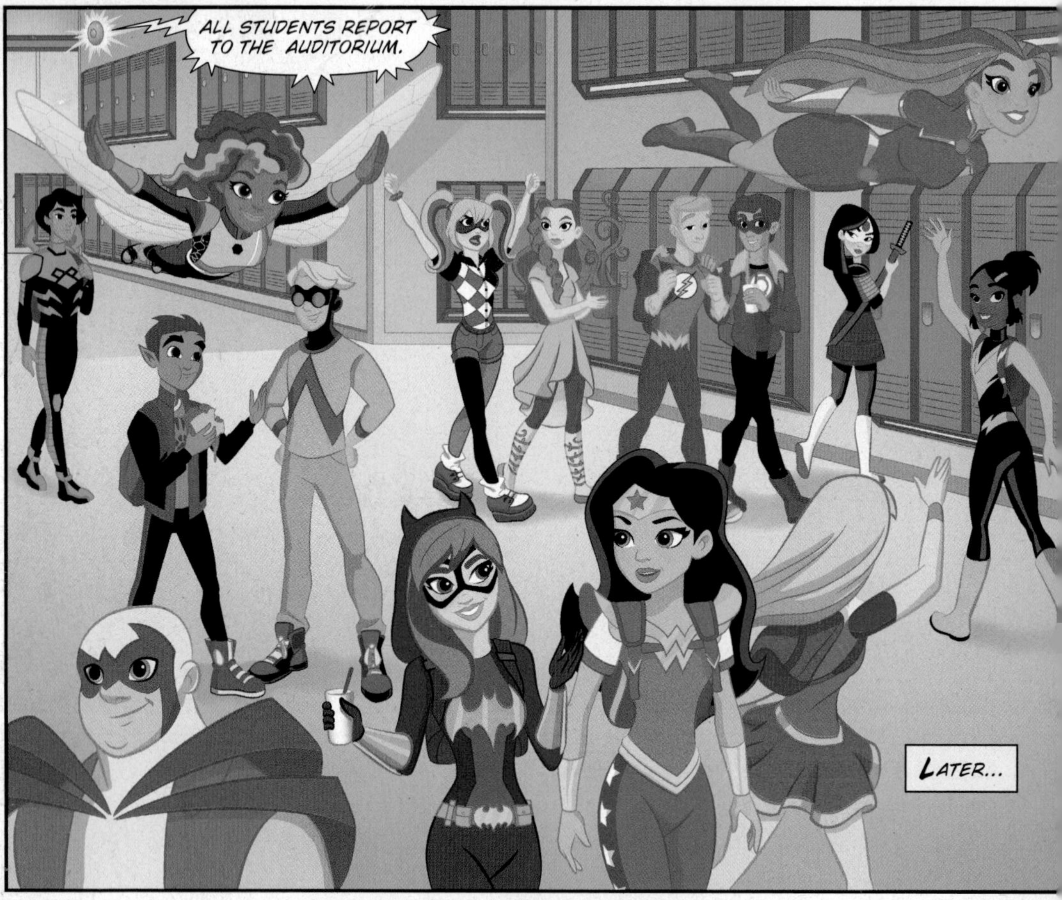
ALL STUDENTS REPORT TO THE AUDITORIUM.
LATER...

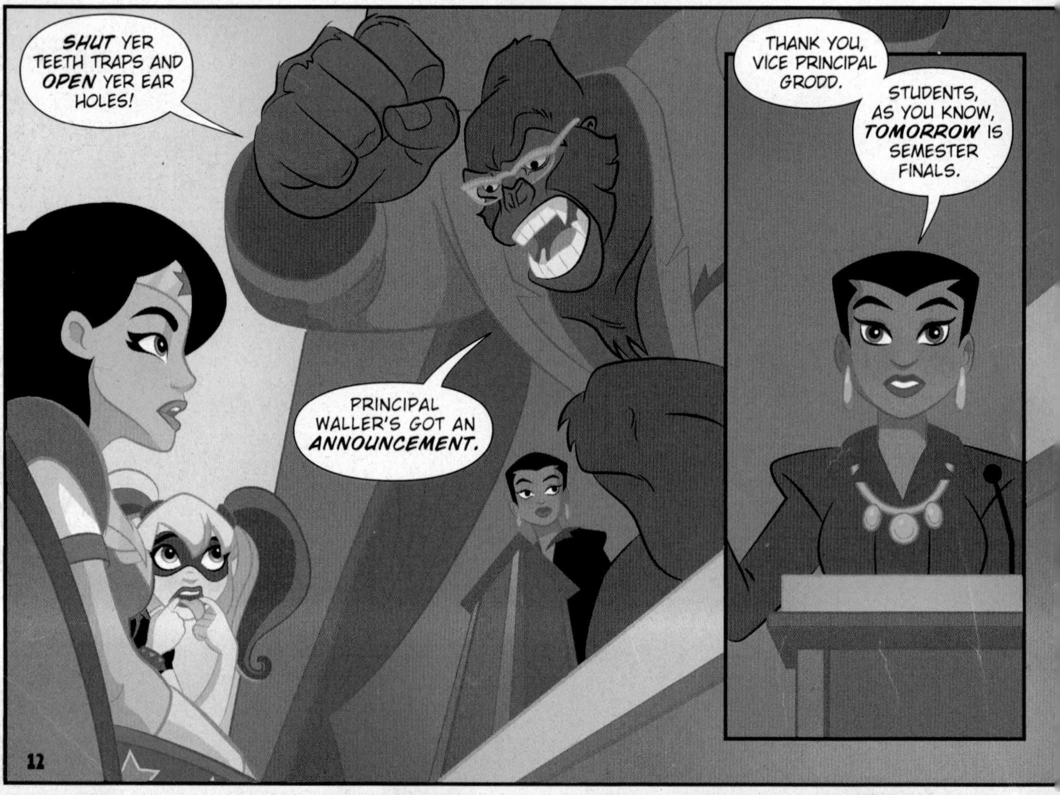
SHUT YER TEETH TRAPS AND OPEN YER EAR HOLES!
PRINCIPAL WALLER'S GOT AN ANNOUNCEMENT.
THANK YOU, VICE PRINCIPAL GRODD.
STUDENTS, AS YOU KNOW, TOMORROW IS SEMESTER FINALS.

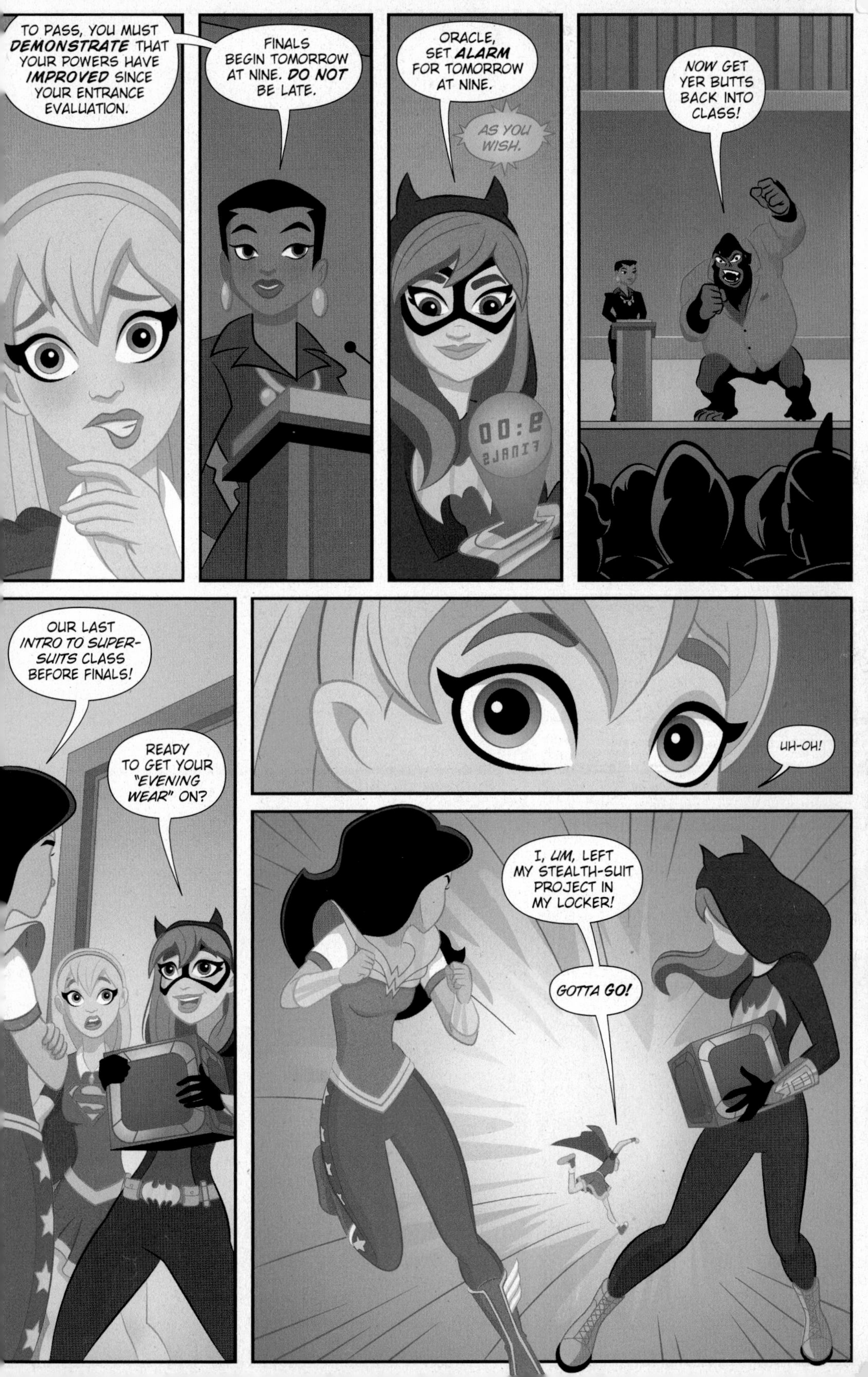
TO PASS, YOU MUST DEMONSTRATE THAT YOUR POWERS HAVE IMPROVED SINCE YOUR ENTRANCE EVALUATION.
FINALS BEGIN TOMORROW AT NINE. DO NOT BE LATE.
ORACLE, SET ALARM FOR TOMORROW AT NINE.
AS YOU WISH.
9:00 FINALS
NOW GET YER BUTTS BACK INTO CLASS!
OUR LAST INTRO TO SUPER-SUITS CLASS BEFORE FINALS!
READY TO GET YOUR "EVENING WEAR" ON?
UH-OH!
I, UM, LEFT MY STEALTH-SUIT PROJECT IN MY LOCKER!
GOTTA GO!

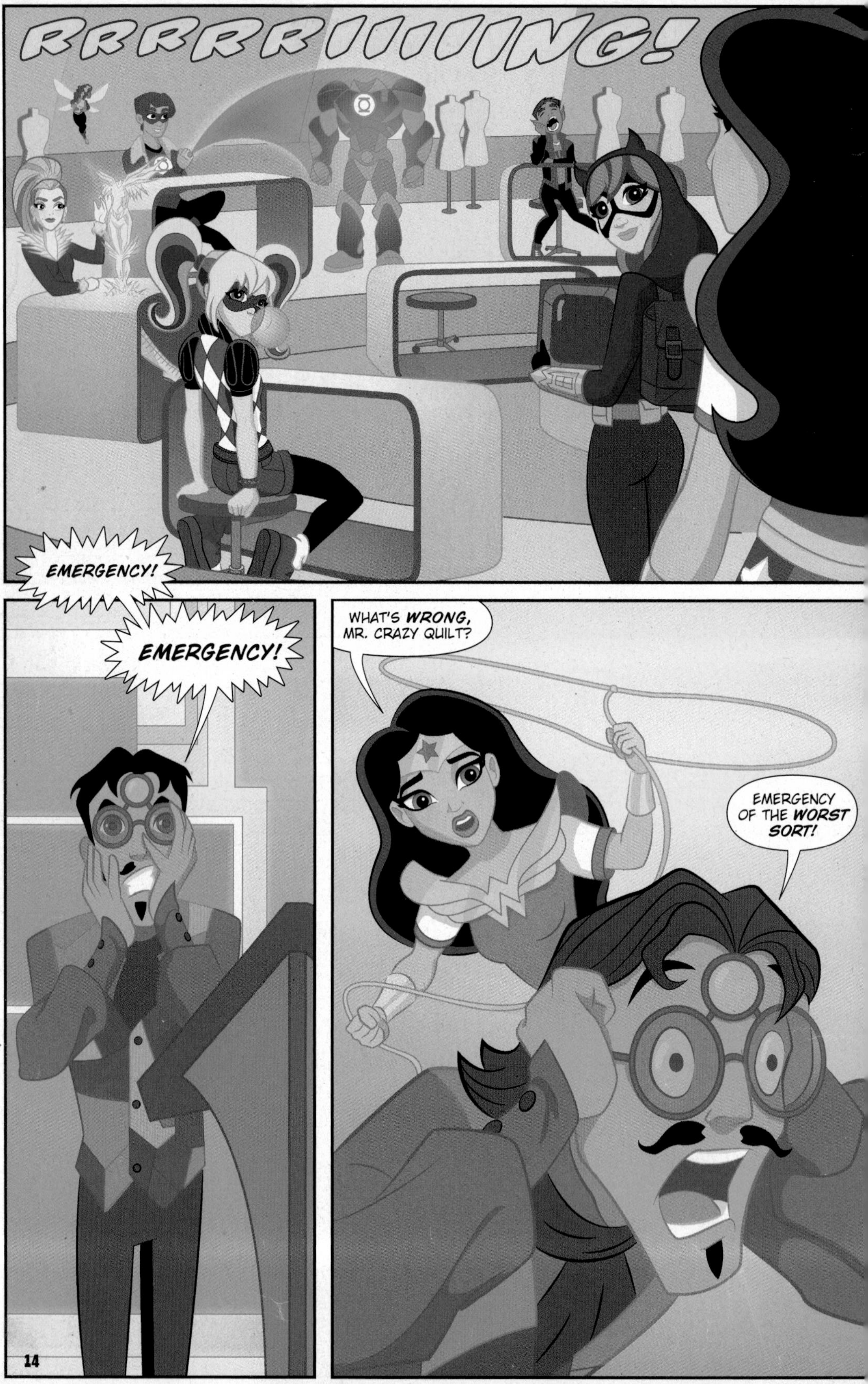
RRRRRIIIIIING!
EMERGENCY!
EMERGENCY!
WHAT'S **WRONG**, MR. CRAZY QUILT?
EMERGENCY OF THE **WORST** SORT!

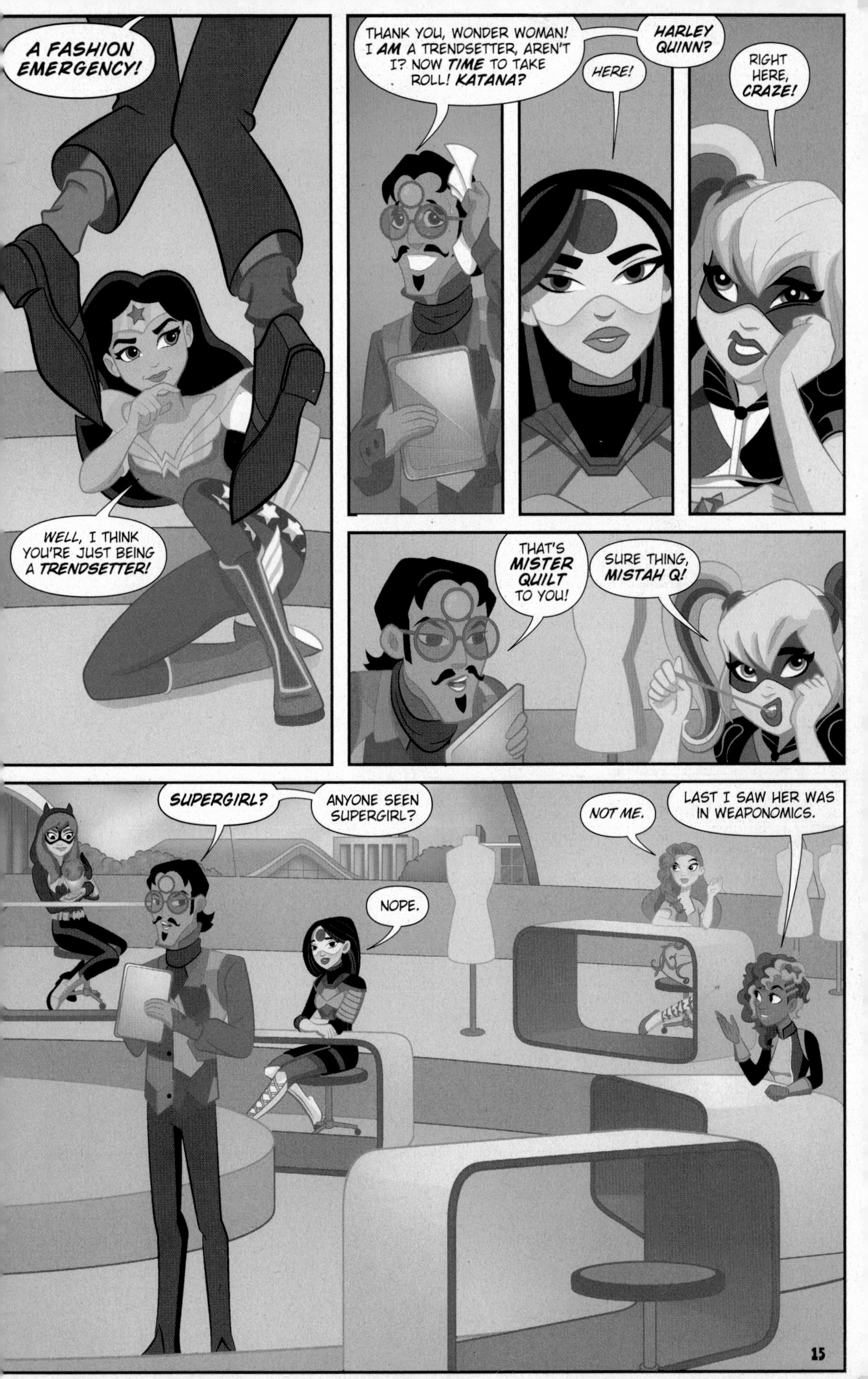
A FASHION EMERGENCY!
WELL, I THINK YOU'RE JUST BEING A TRENDSETTER!
THANK YOU, WONDER WOMAN! I AM A TRENDSETTER, AREN'T I? NOW TIME TO TAKE ROLL! KATANA?
HERE!
HARLEY QUINN?
RIGHT HERE, CRAZE!
THAT'S MISTER QUILT TO YOU!
SURE THING, MISTAH Q!
SUPERGIRL?
ANYONE SEEN SUPERGIRL?
NOPE.
NOT ME.
LAST I SAW HER WAS IN WEAPONOMICS.

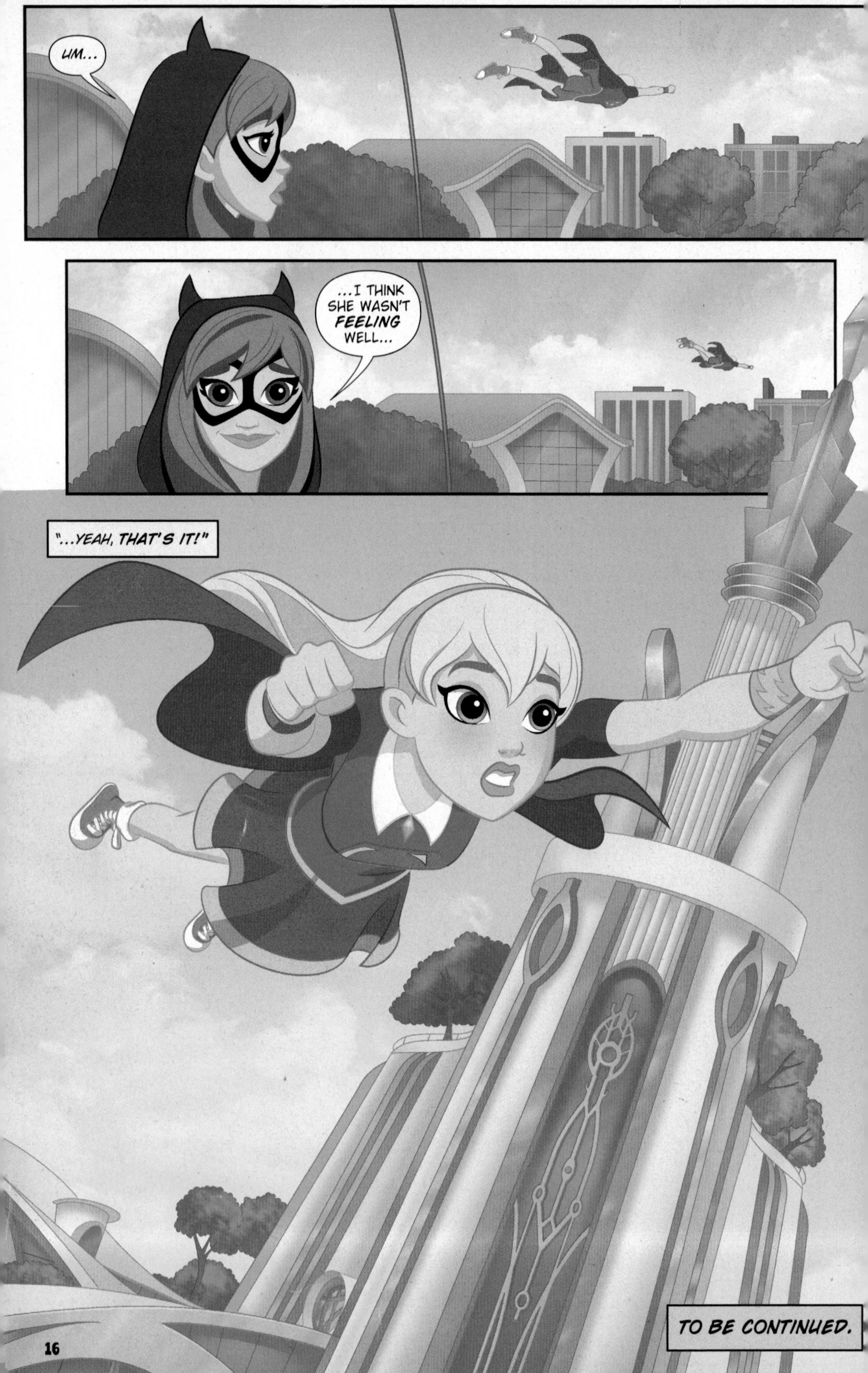
UM...
...I THINK SHE WASN'T FEELING WELL...
"...YEAH, THAT'S IT!"
TO BE CONTINUED.

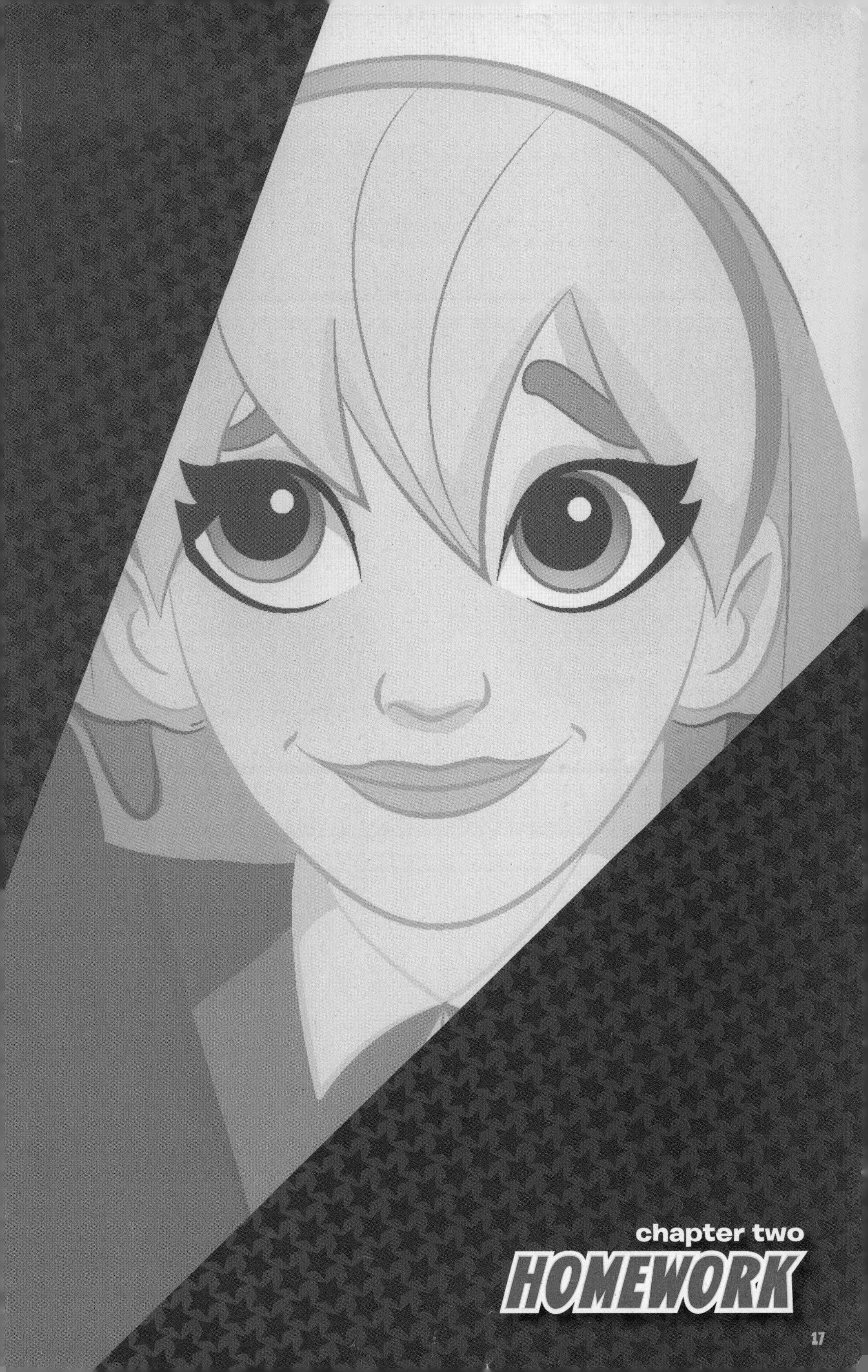

chapter two
HOMEWORK

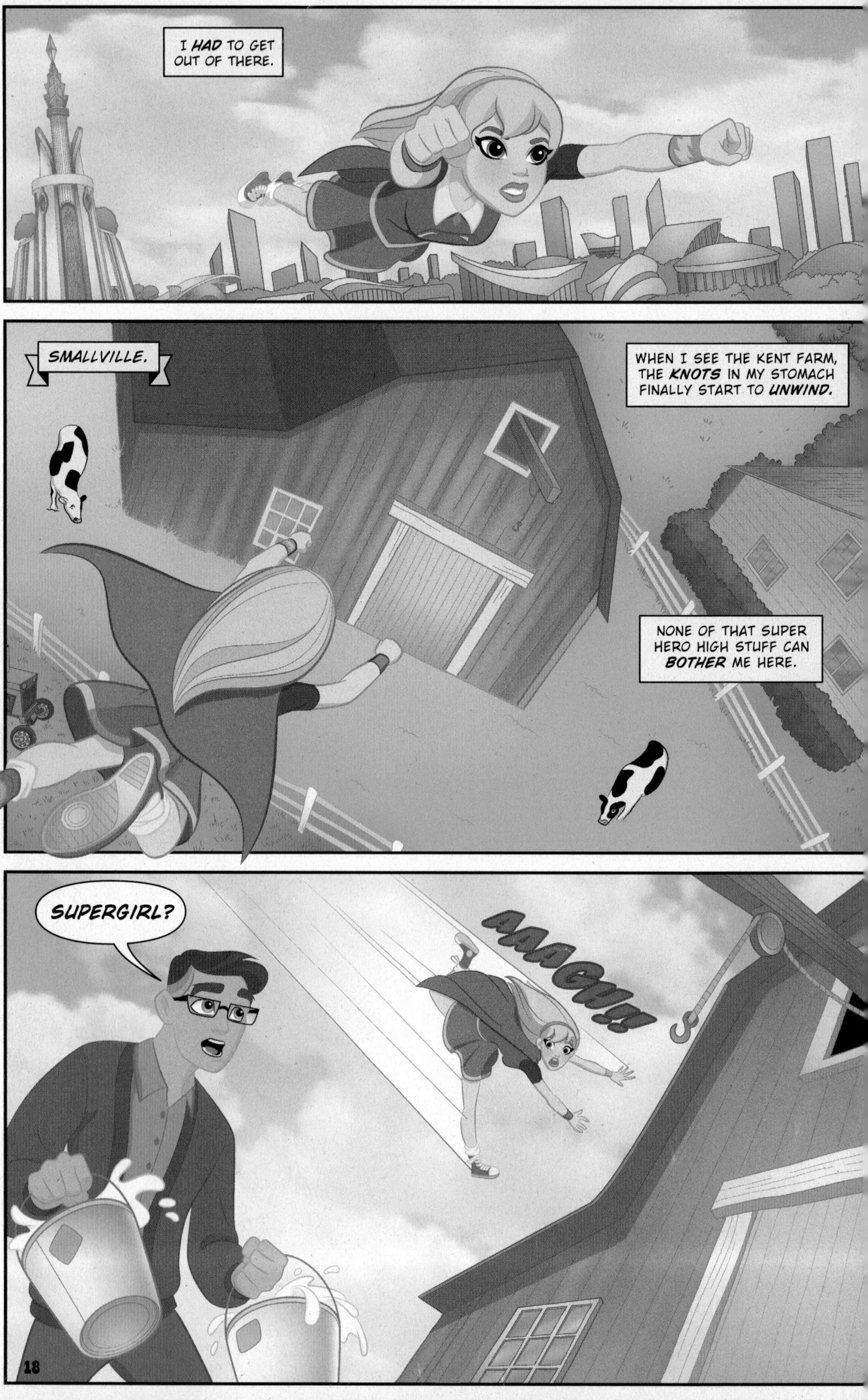
I HAD TO GET OUT OF THERE.
SMALLVILLE.
WHEN I SEE THE KENT FARM, THE KNOTS IN MY STOMACH FINALLY START TO UNWIND.
NONE OF THAT SUPER HERO HIGH STUFF CAN BOTHER ME HERE.
SUPERGIRL?
AAAGH!!

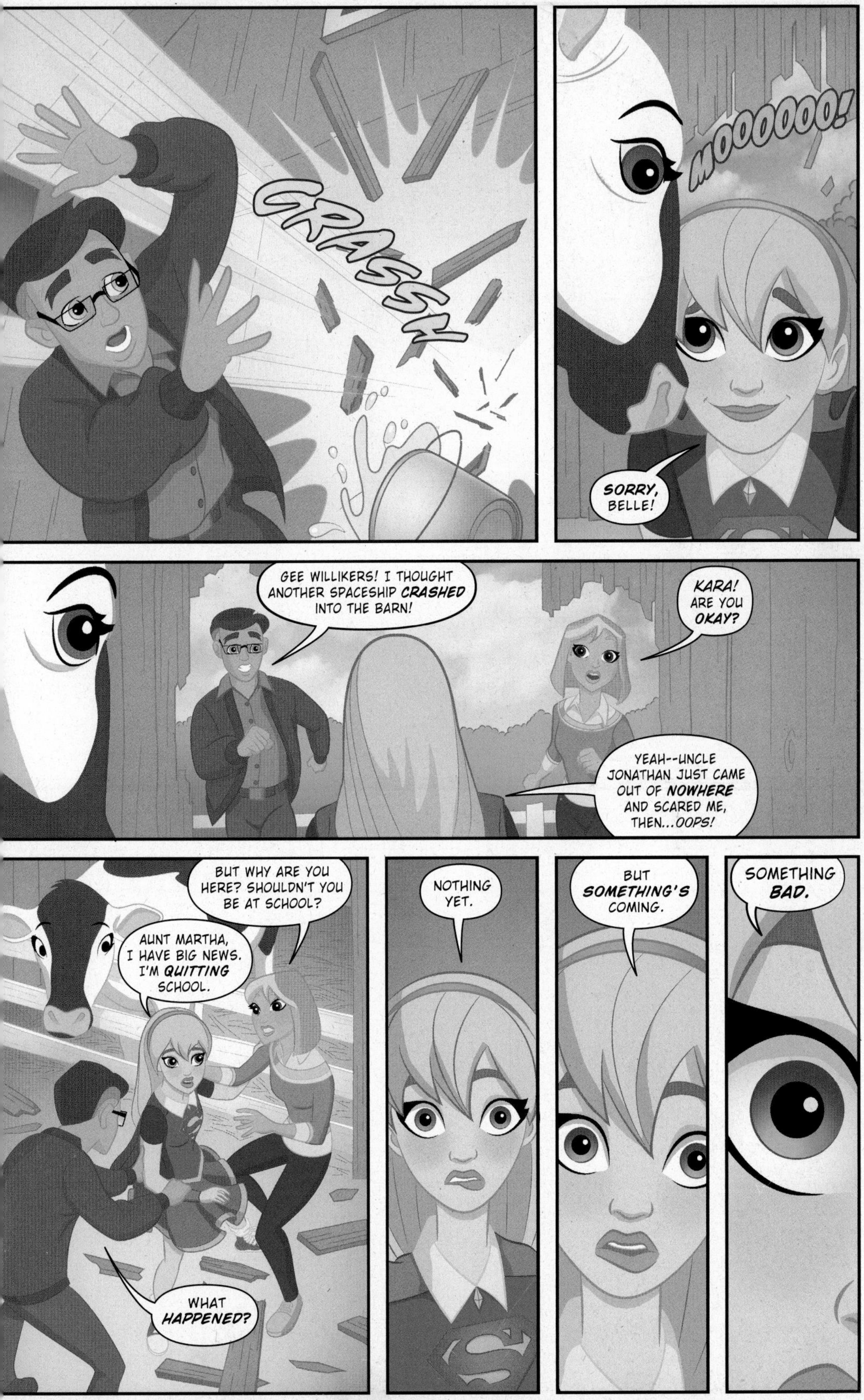
CRASSH
MOOOOOO!
SORRY, BELLE!
GEE WILLIKERS! I THOUGHT ANOTHER SPACESHIP CRASHED INTO THE BARN!
KARA! ARE YOU OKAY?
YEAH--UNCLE JONATHAN JUST CAME OUT OF NOWHERE AND SCARED ME, THEN...OOPS!
BUT WHY ARE YOU HERE? SHOULDN'T YOU BE AT SCHOOL?
AUNT MARTHA, I HAVE BIG NEWS. I'M QUITTING SCHOOL.
WHAT HAPPENED?
NOTHING YET.
BUT SOMETHING'S COMING.
SOMETHING BAD.

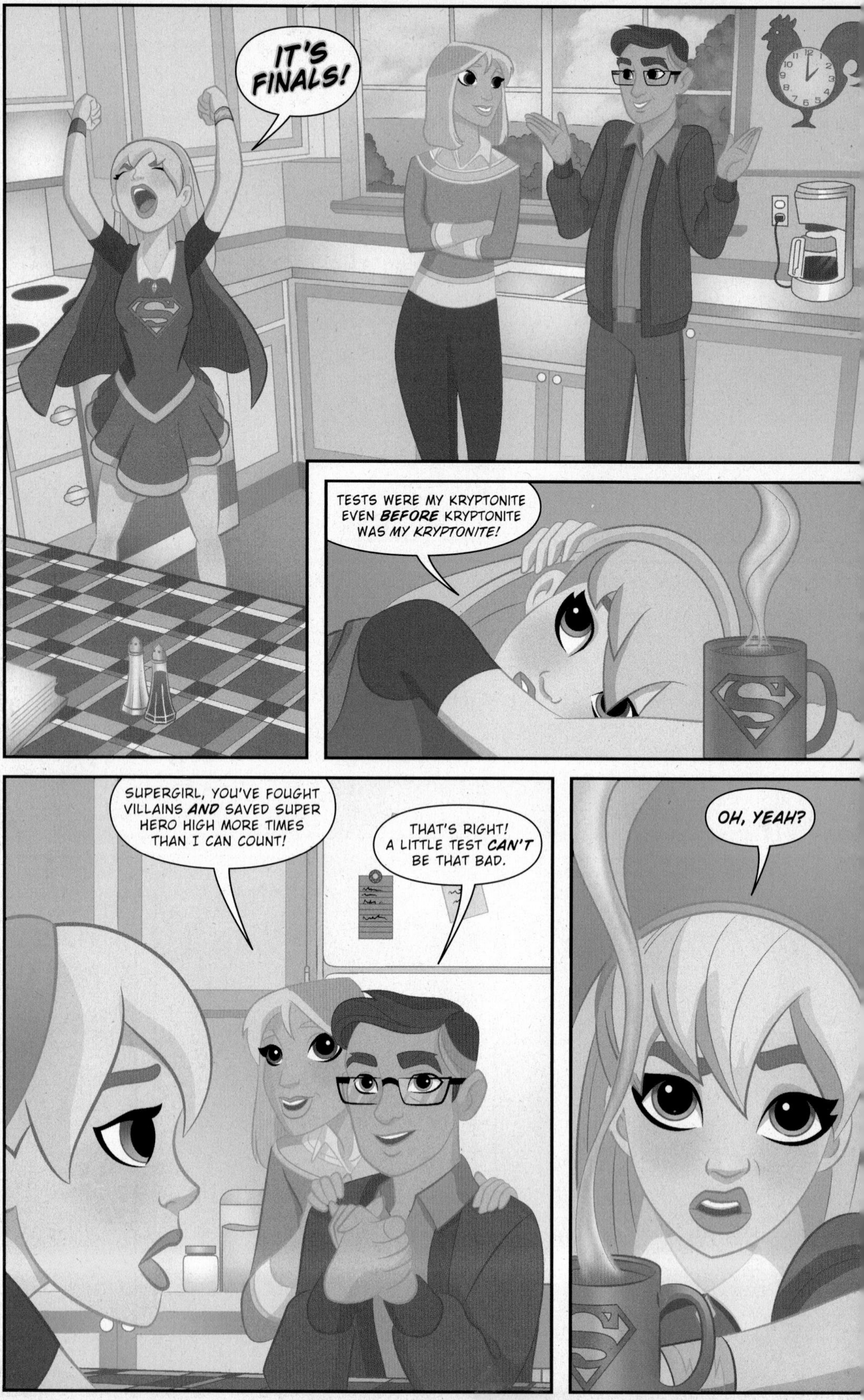
IT'S FINALS!
TESTS WERE MY KRYPTONITE EVEN BEFORE KRYPTONITE WAS MY KRYPTONITE!
SUPERGIRL, YOU'VE FOUGHT VILLAINS AND SAVED SUPER HERO HIGH MORE TIMES THAN I CAN COUNT!
THAT'S RIGHT! A LITTLE TEST CAN'T BE THAT BAD.
OH, YEAH?

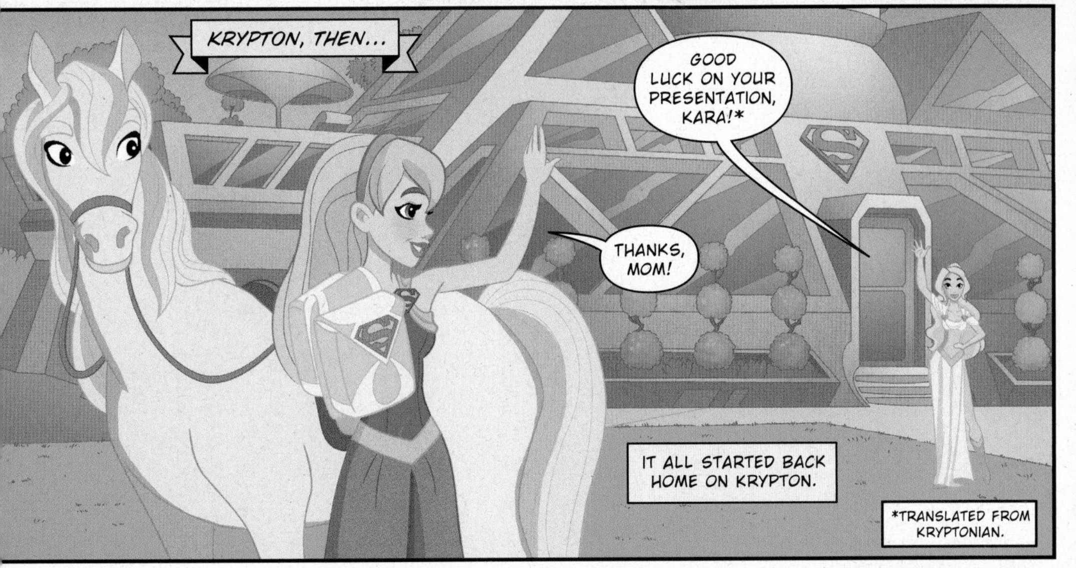
KRYPTON, THEN...
GOOD LUCK ON YOUR PRESENTATION, KARA!*
THANKS, MOM!
IT ALL STARTED BACK HOME ON KRYPTON.
*TRANSLATED FROM KRYPTONIAN.

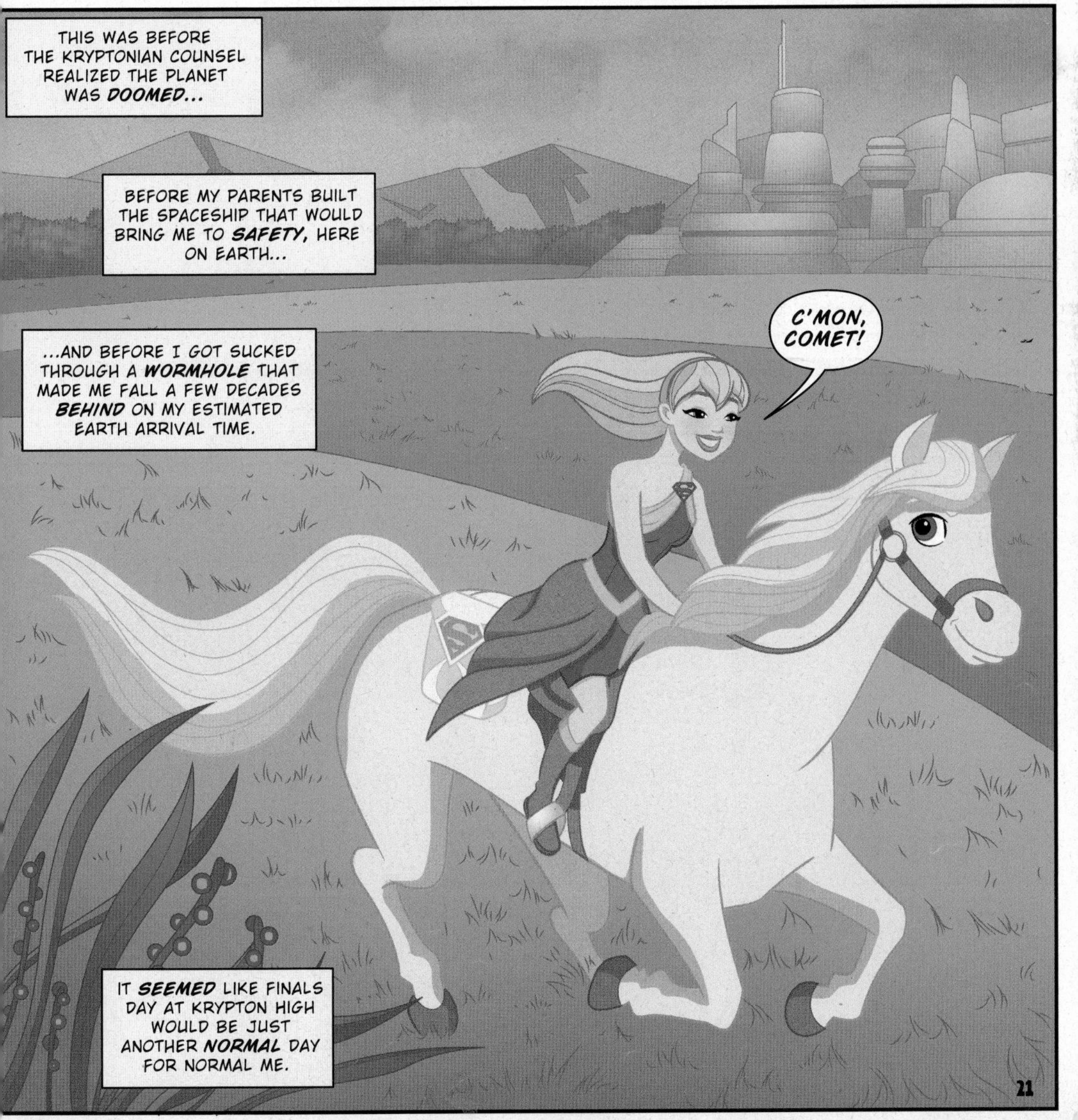
THIS WAS BEFORE THE KRYPTONIAN COUNSEL REALIZED THE PLANET WAS DOOMED...
BEFORE MY PARENTS BUILT THE SPACESHIP THAT WOULD BRING ME TO SAFETY, HERE ON EARTH...
...AND BEFORE I GOT SUCKED THROUGH A WORMHOLE THAT MADE ME FALL A FEW DECADES BEHIND ON MY ESTIMATED EARTH ARRIVAL TIME.
C'MON, COMET!
IT SEEMED LIKE FINALS DAY AT KRYPTON HIGH WOULD BE JUST ANOTHER NORMAL DAY FOR NORMAL ME.

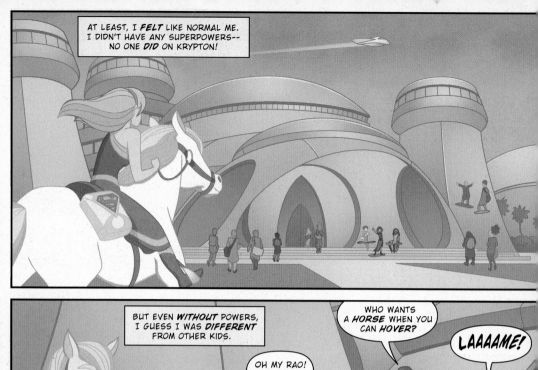

AT LEAST, I *FELT* LIKE NORMAL ME. I DIDN'T HAVE ANY SUPERPOWERS-- NO ONE *DID* ON KRYPTON!

BUT EVEN *WITHOUT* POWERS, I GUESS I WAS *DIFFERENT* FROM OTHER KIDS.

OH MY RAO! *LOOK* AT KARA!

WHO WANTS A *HORSE* WHEN YOU CAN *HOVER?*

LAAAAME!

HEY, KARA, EORX 8999 TELECOMMUNICATED. THEY WANT THEIR MODE OF TRANSPORTATION BACK!

HA HA HA HA HA!

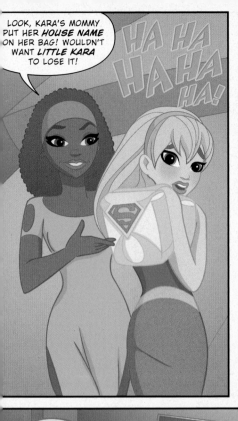

LOOK, KARA'S MOMMY PUT HER *HOUSE NAME* ON HER BAG! WOULDN'T WANT *LITTLE KARA* TO LOSE IT!

HA HA HA HA HA!

WHAT A *WEAKLING!*

WHOA!

MAMA'S GIRL!

RRRRRRING!

SPLASH

YOU'LL BE UP *FIRST,* KARA.

SORRY I'M LATE!

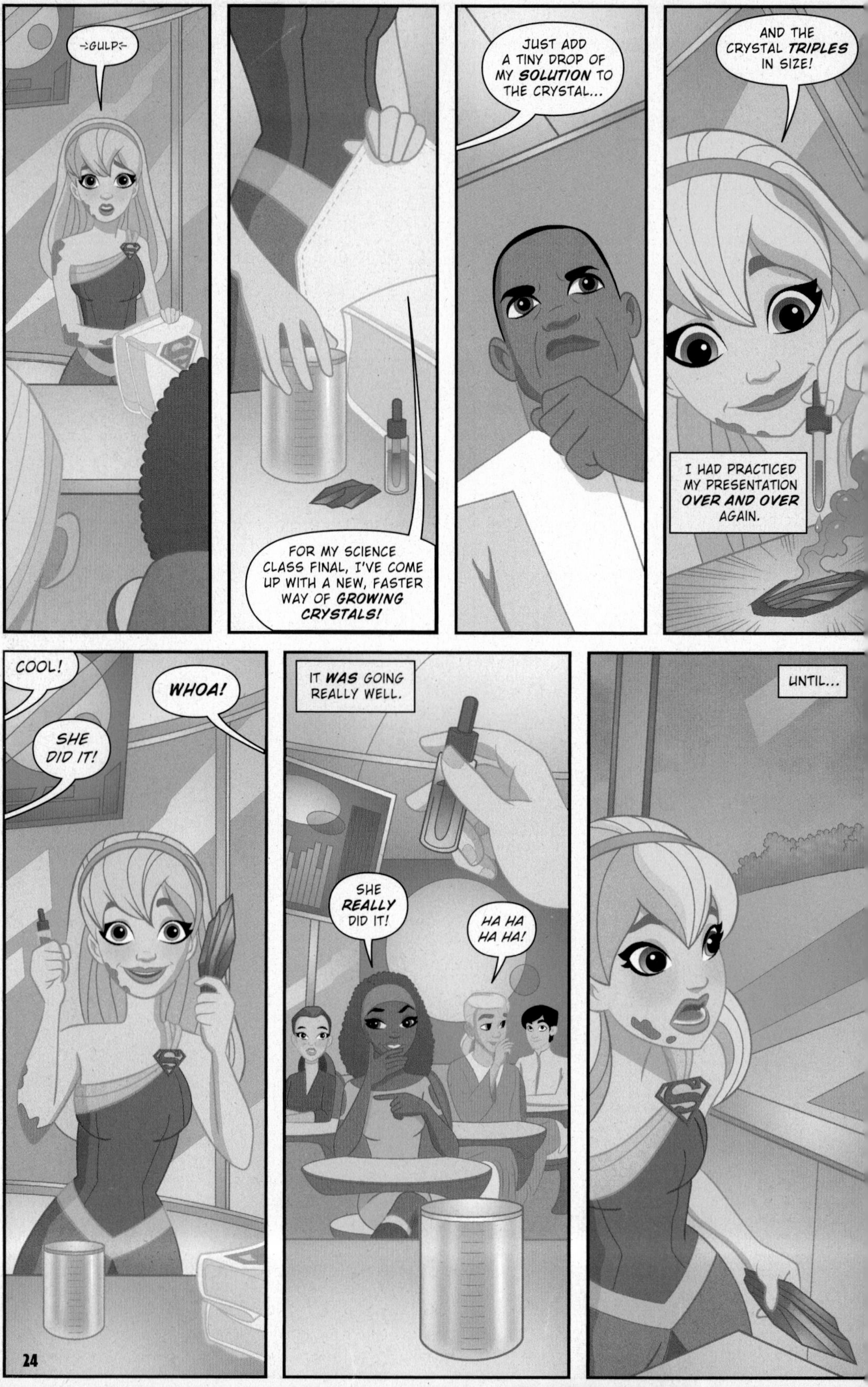

-GULP-
FOR MY SCIENCE CLASS FINAL, I'VE COME UP WITH A NEW, FASTER WAY OF GROWING CRYSTALS!
JUST ADD A TINY DROP OF MY SOLUTION TO THE CRYSTAL...
AND THE CRYSTAL TRIPLES IN SIZE!
I HAD PRACTICED MY PRESENTATION OVER AND OVER AGAIN.
COOL!
WHOA!
SHE DID IT!
IT WAS GOING REALLY WELL.
SHE REALLY DID IT!
HA HA HA HA!
UNTIL...

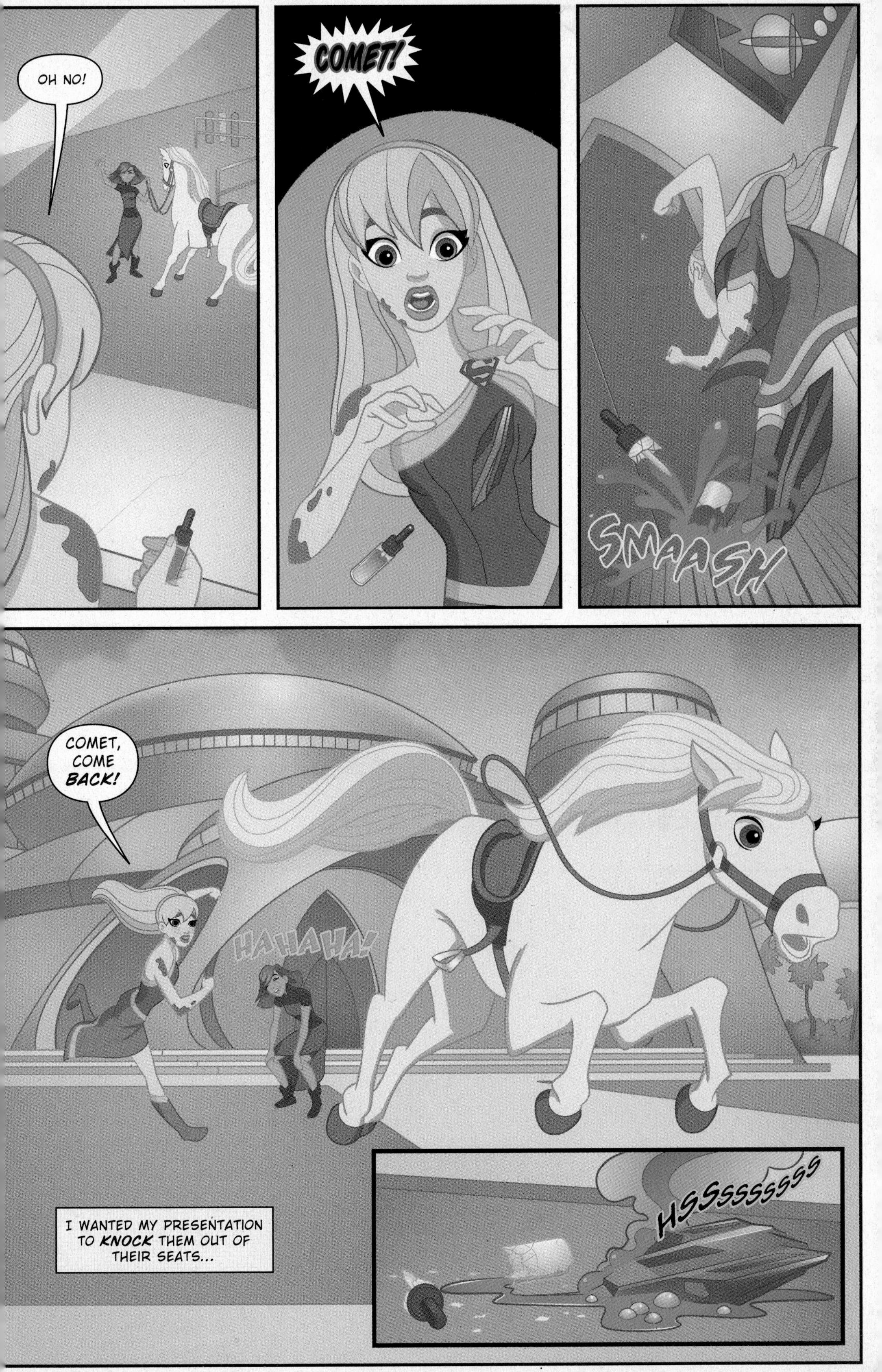
OH NO!
COMET!
SMAASH
COMET, COME BACK!
HAHAHA!
I WANTED MY PRESENTATION TO KNOCK THEM OUT OF THEIR SEATS...
HSSSSSSSSS

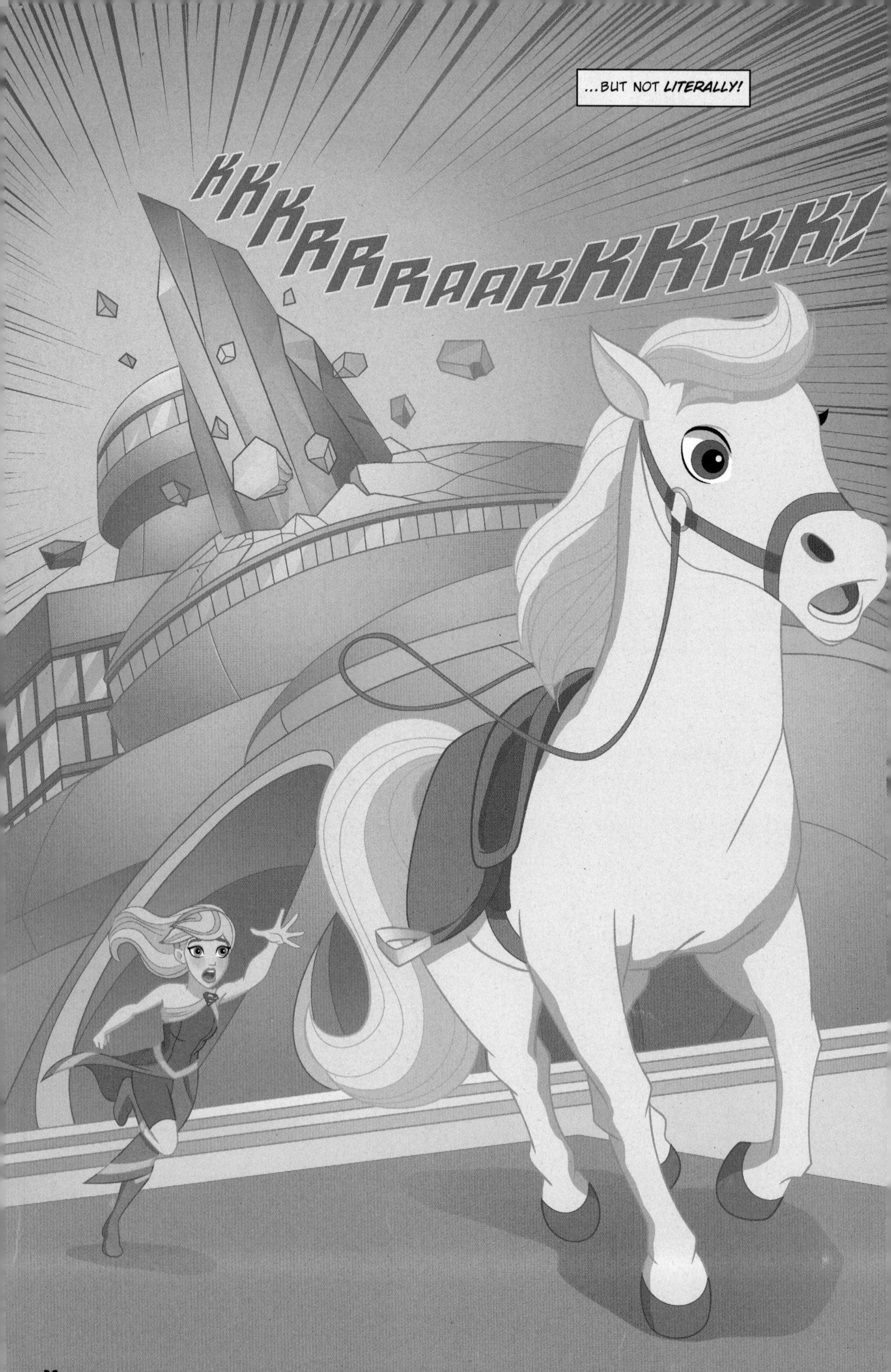
...BUT NOT LITERALLY!
KKKRRRRAAKKKKK!

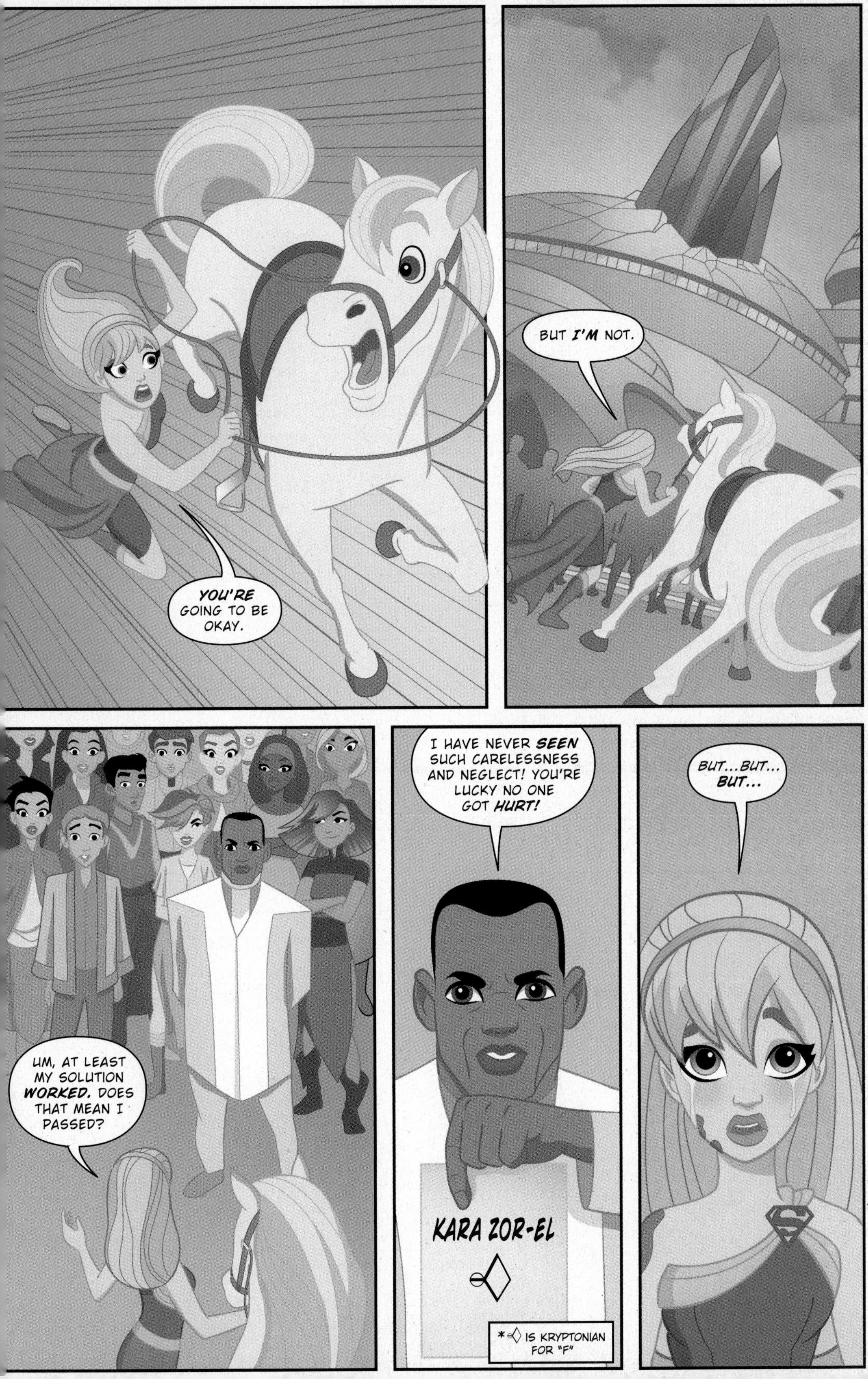
YOU'RE GOING TO BE OKAY.
BUT I'M NOT.
UM, AT LEAST MY SOLUTION WORKED. DOES THAT MEAN I PASSED?
I HAVE NEVER SEEN SUCH CARELESSNESS AND NEGLECT! YOU'RE LUCKY NO ONE GOT HURT!
KARA ZOR-EL
* IS KRYPTONIAN FOR "F"
BUT...BUT... BUT...

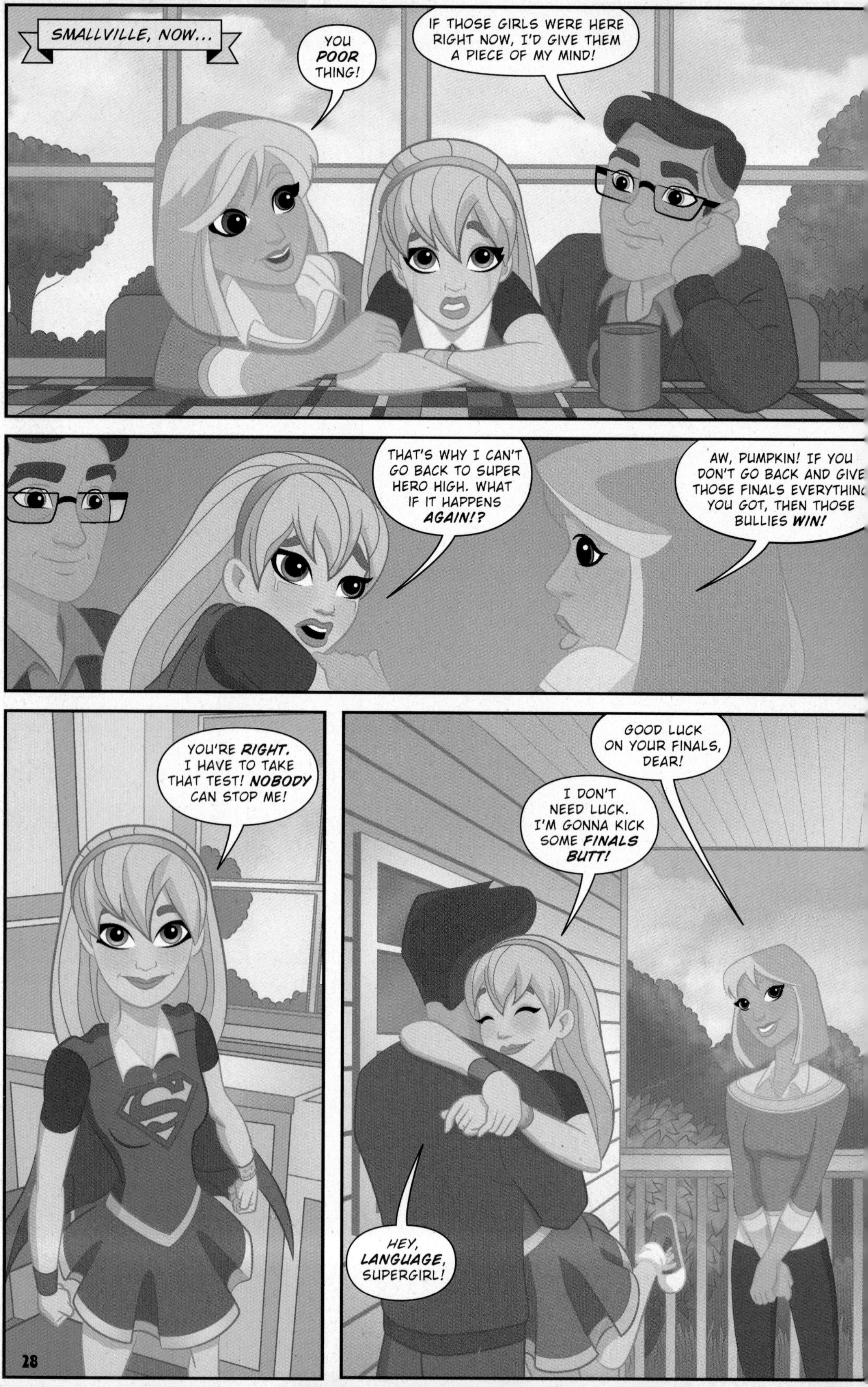
SMALLVILLE, NOW...
YOU POOR THING!
IF THOSE GIRLS WERE HERE RIGHT NOW, I'D GIVE THEM A PIECE OF MY MIND!
THAT'S WHY I CAN'T GO BACK TO SUPER HERO HIGH. WHAT IF IT HAPPENS AGAIN!?
AW, PUMPKIN! IF YOU DON'T GO BACK AND GIVE THOSE FINALS EVERYTHING YOU GOT, THEN THOSE BULLIES WIN!
YOU'RE RIGHT. I HAVE TO TAKE THAT TEST! NOBODY CAN STOP ME!
GOOD LUCK ON YOUR FINALS, DEAR!
I DON'T NEED LUCK. I'M GONNA KICK SOME FINALS BUTT!
HEY, LANGUAGE, SUPERGIRL!

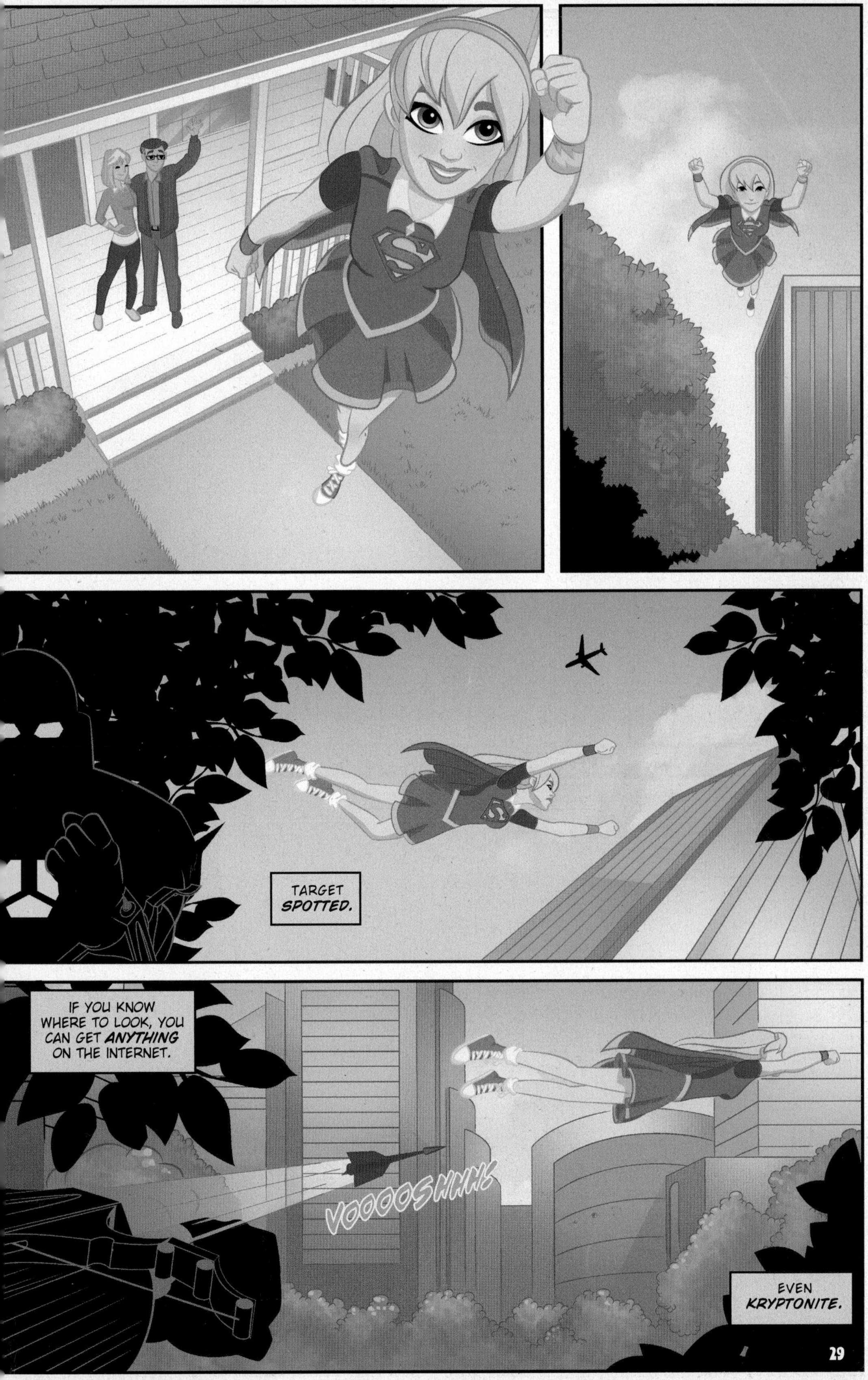
TARGET SPOTTED.
IF YOU KNOW WHERE TO LOOK, YOU CAN GET ANYTHING ON THE INTERNET.
VOOOOSHHH!
EVEN KRYPTONITE.

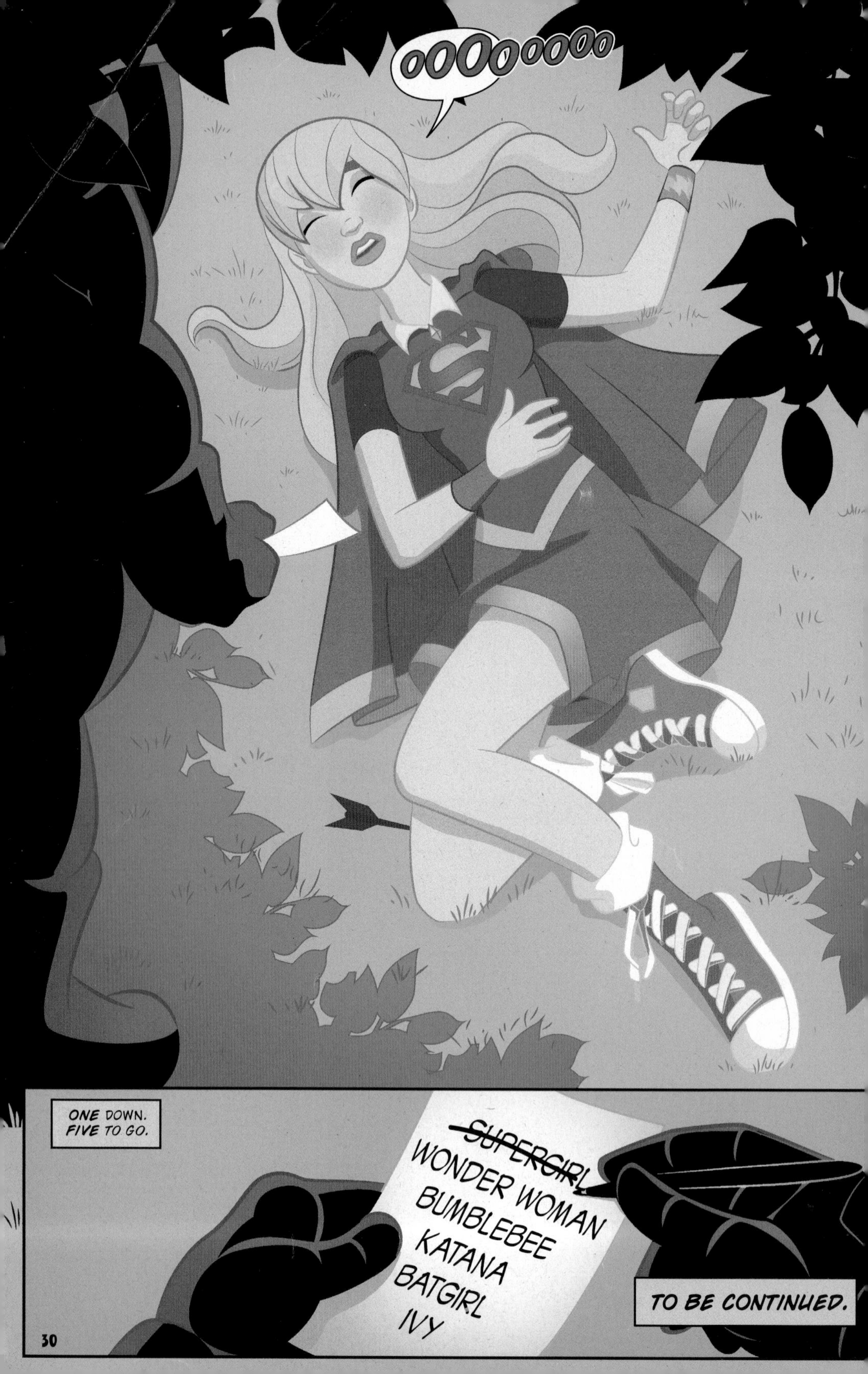
OOOOOOOO
ONE DOWN. FIVE TO GO.
SUPERGIRL
WONDER WOMAN
BUMBLEBEE
KATANA
BATGIRL
IVY
TO BE CONTINUED.

chapter three

GROWING UP

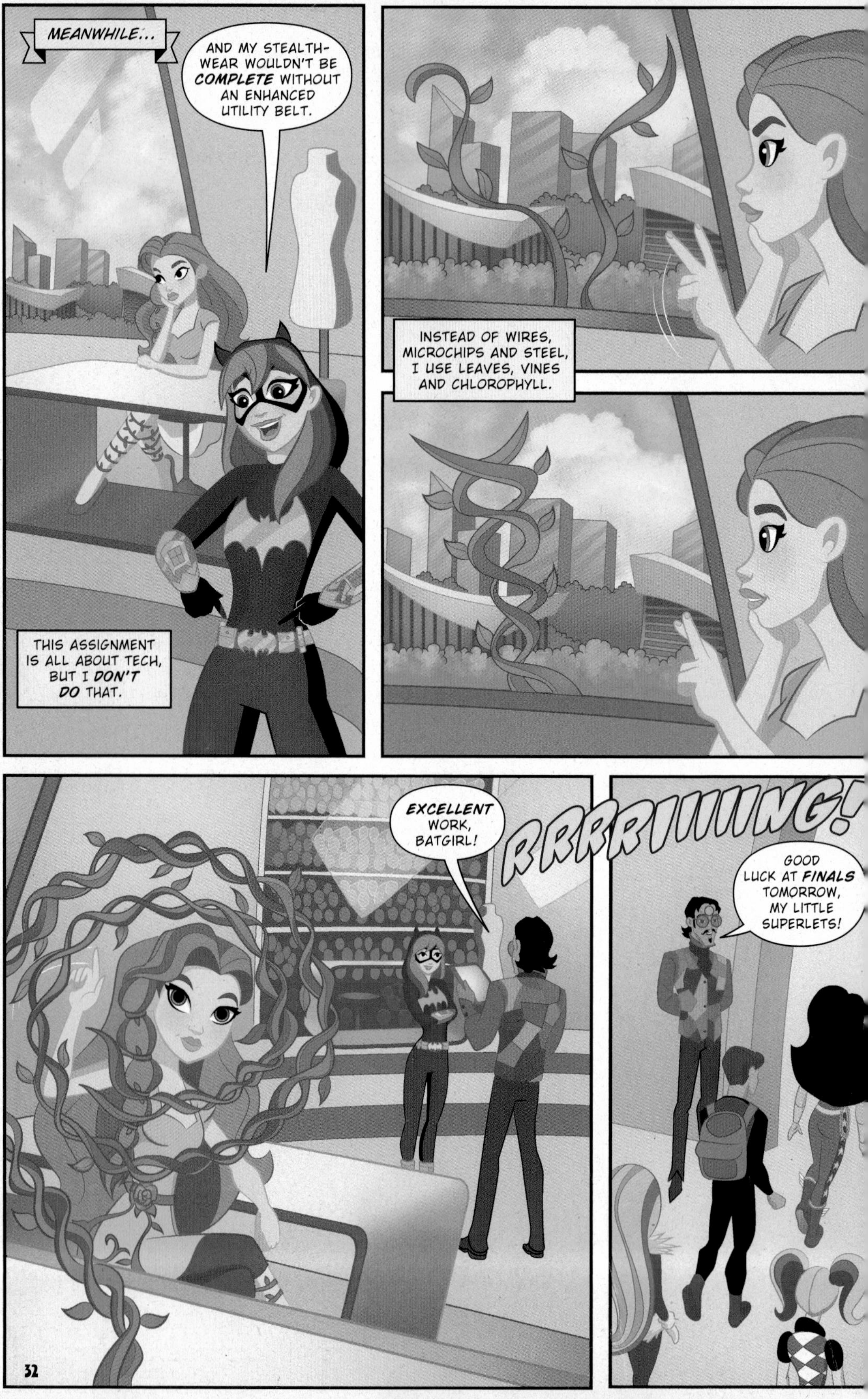

MEANWHILE...
AND MY STEALTH-WEAR WOULDN'T BE ***COMPLETE*** WITHOUT AN ENHANCED UTILITY BELT.
THIS ASSIGNMENT IS ALL ABOUT TECH, BUT I ***DON'T DO*** THAT.
INSTEAD OF WIRES, MICROCHIPS AND STEEL, I USE LEAVES, VINES AND CHLOROPHYLL.
EXCELLENT WORK, BATGIRL!
RRRRIIIIING!
GOOD LUCK AT ***FINALS*** TOMORROW, MY LITTLE SUPERLETS!

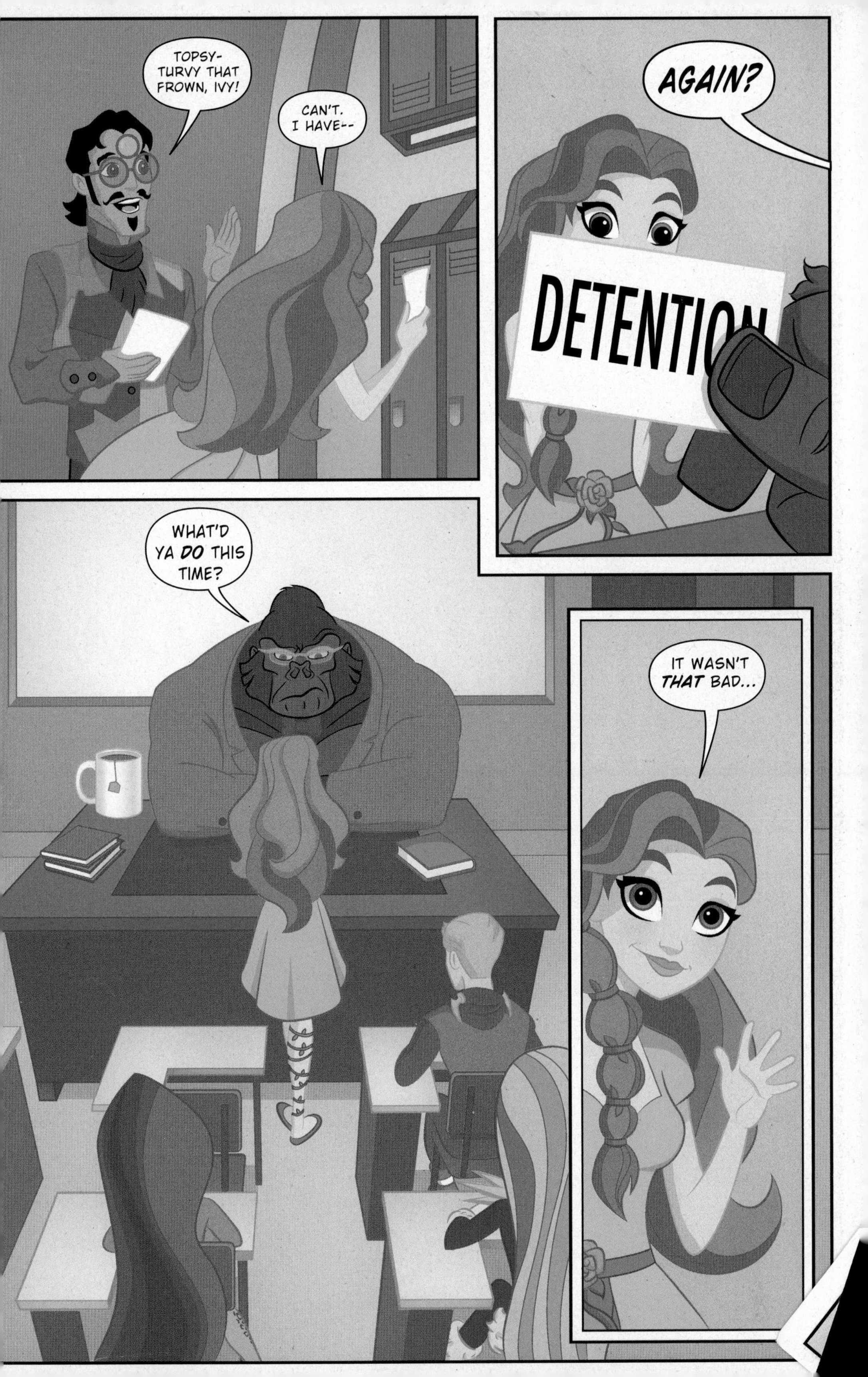
TOPSY-TURVY THAT FROWN, IVY!
CAN'T. I HAVE--
AGAIN?
DETENTION
WHAT'D YA DO THIS TIME?
IT WASN'T THAT BAD...

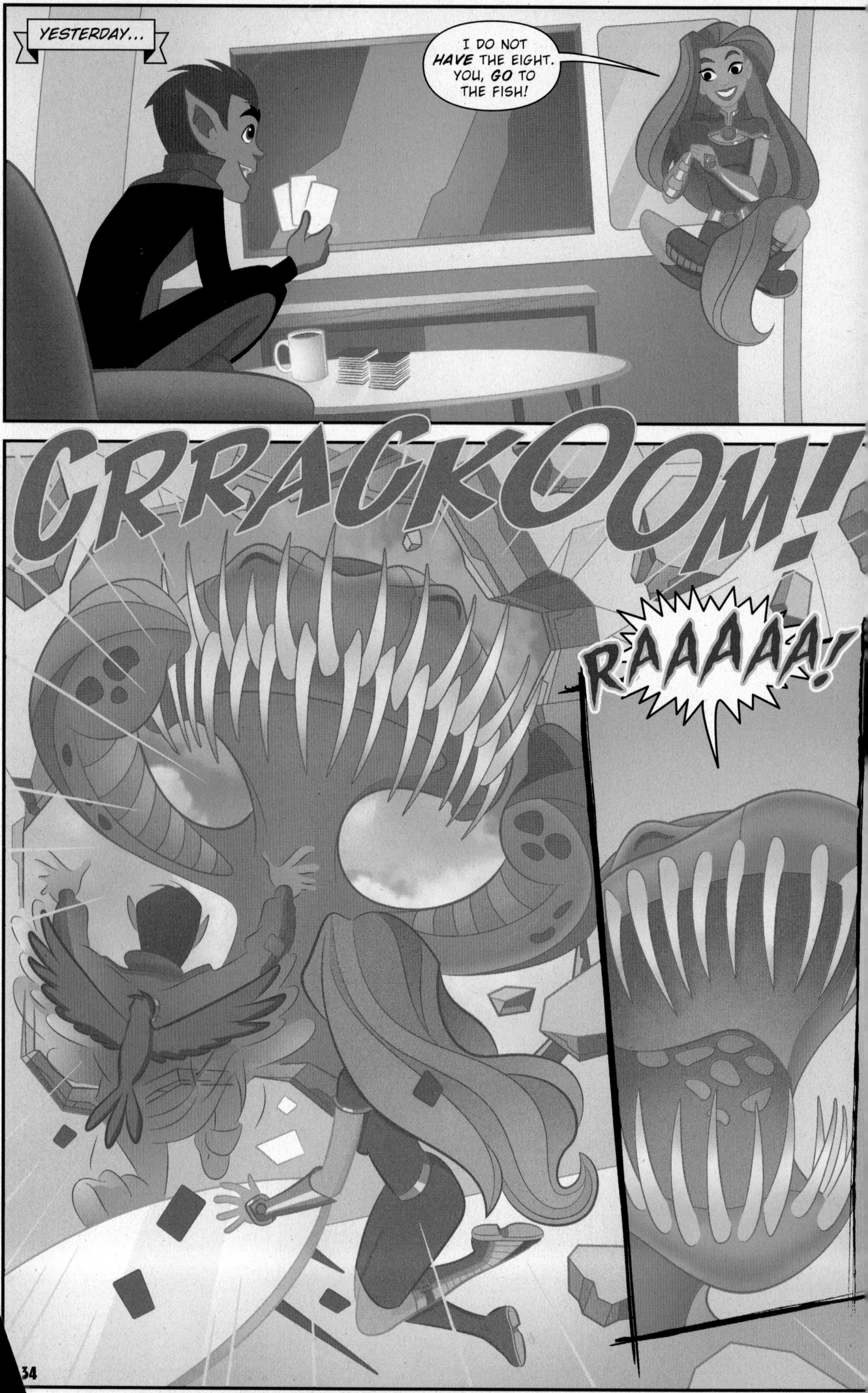
YESTERDAY...
I DO NOT HAVE THE EIGHT. YOU, GO TO THE FISH!
CRRACKOOM!
RAAAAAA!

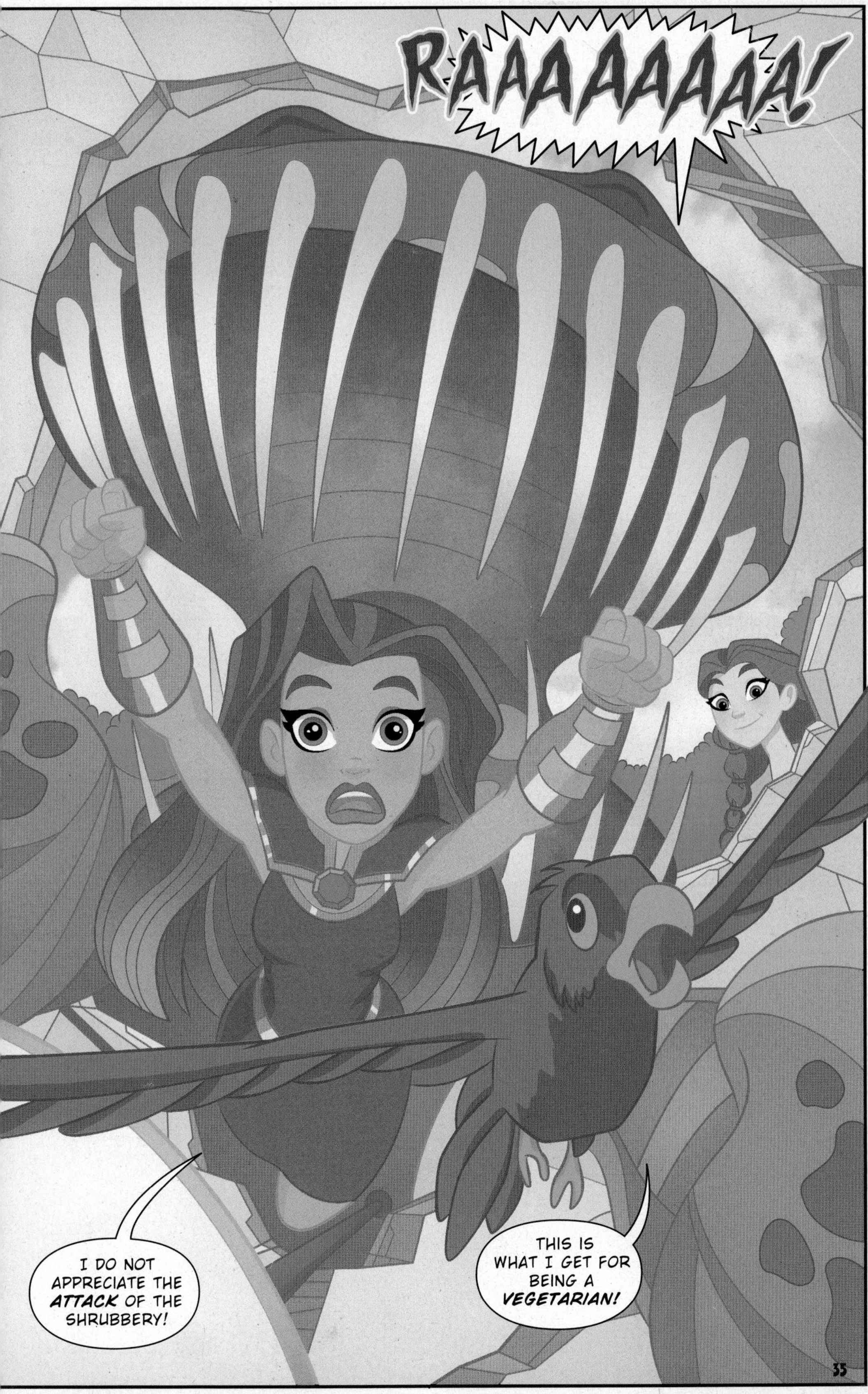
RAAAAAAAA!
I DO NOT APPRECIATE THE ATTACK OF THE SHRUBBERY!
THIS IS WHAT I GET FOR BEING A VEGETARIAN!

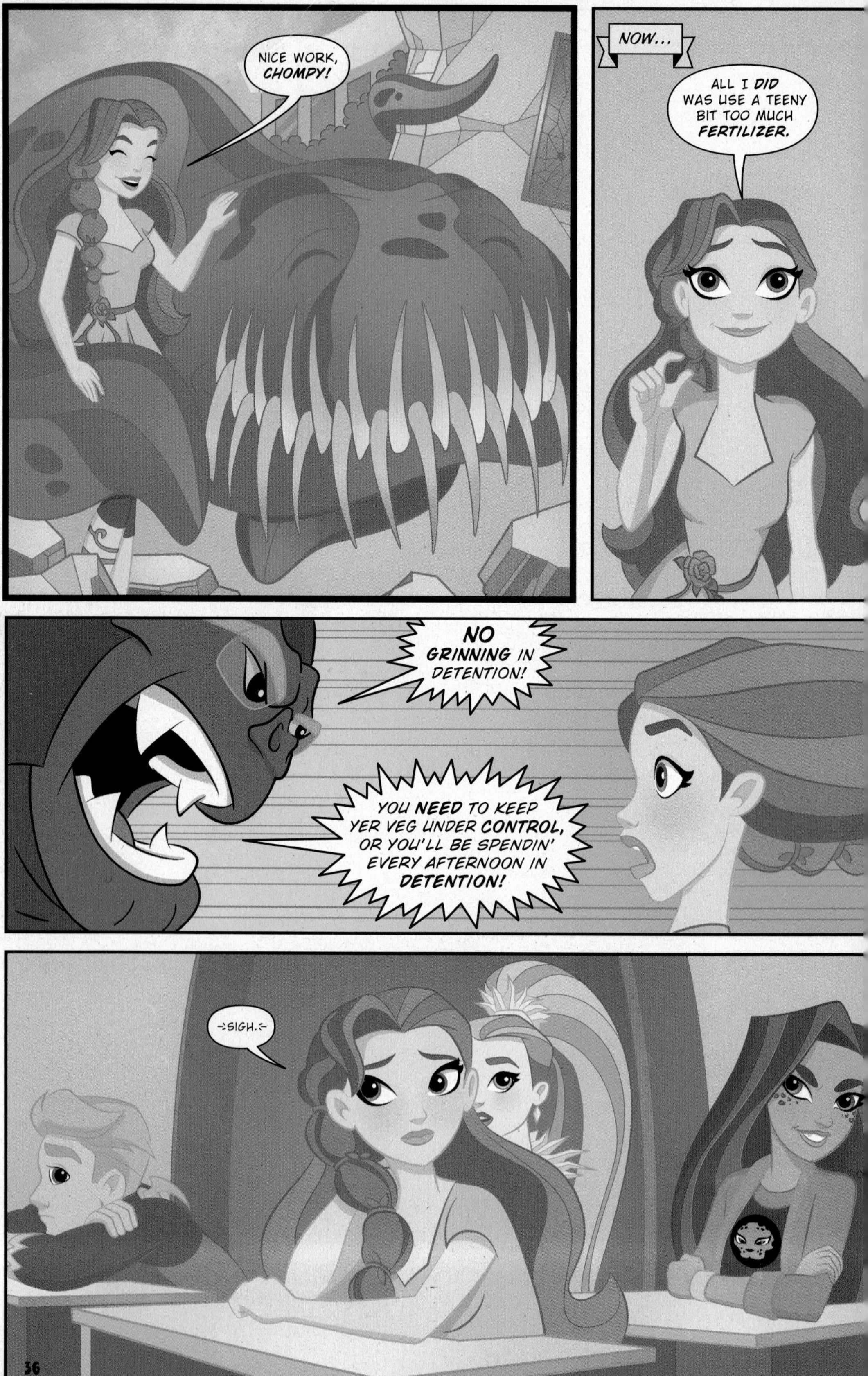
NICE WORK, CHOMPY!
NOW...
ALL I DID WAS USE A TEENY BIT TOO MUCH FERTILIZER.
NO GRINNING IN DETENTION!
YOU NEED TO KEEP YER VEG UNDER CONTROL, OR YOU'LL BE SPENDIN' EVERY AFTERNOON IN DETENTION!
-SIGH.-

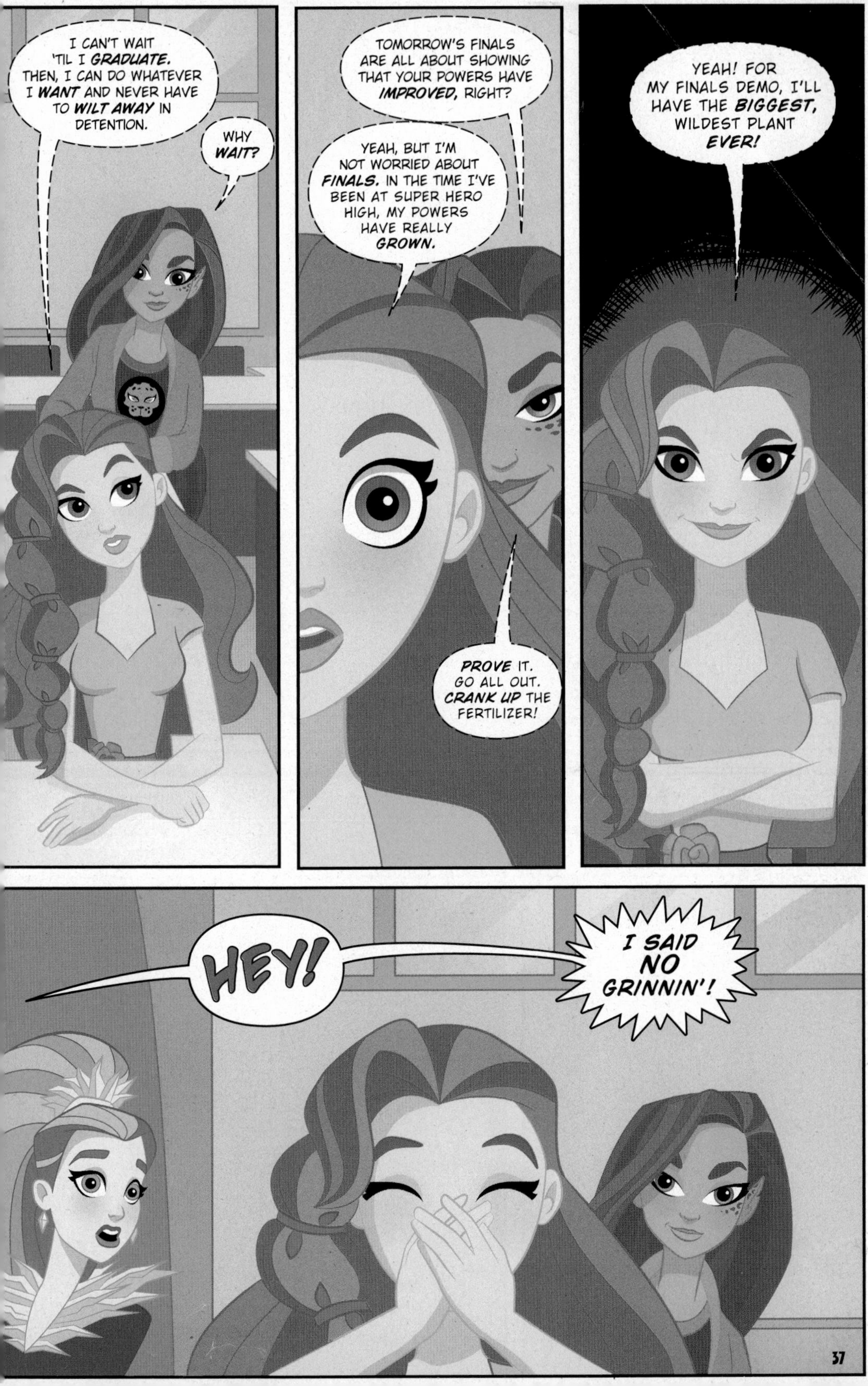
I CAN'T WAIT 'TIL I GRADUATE. THEN, I CAN DO WHATEVER I WANT AND NEVER HAVE TO WILT AWAY IN DETENTION.
WHY WAIT?
TOMORROW'S FINALS ARE ALL ABOUT SHOWING THAT YOUR POWERS HAVE IMPROVED, RIGHT?
YEAH, BUT I'M NOT WORRIED ABOUT FINALS. IN THE TIME I'VE BEEN AT SUPER HERO HIGH, MY POWERS HAVE REALLY GROWN.
PROVE IT. GO ALL OUT. CRANK UP THE FERTILIZER!
YEAH! FOR MY FINALS DEMO, I'LL HAVE THE BIGGEST, WILDEST PLANT EVER!
HEY!
I SAID NO GRINNIN'!

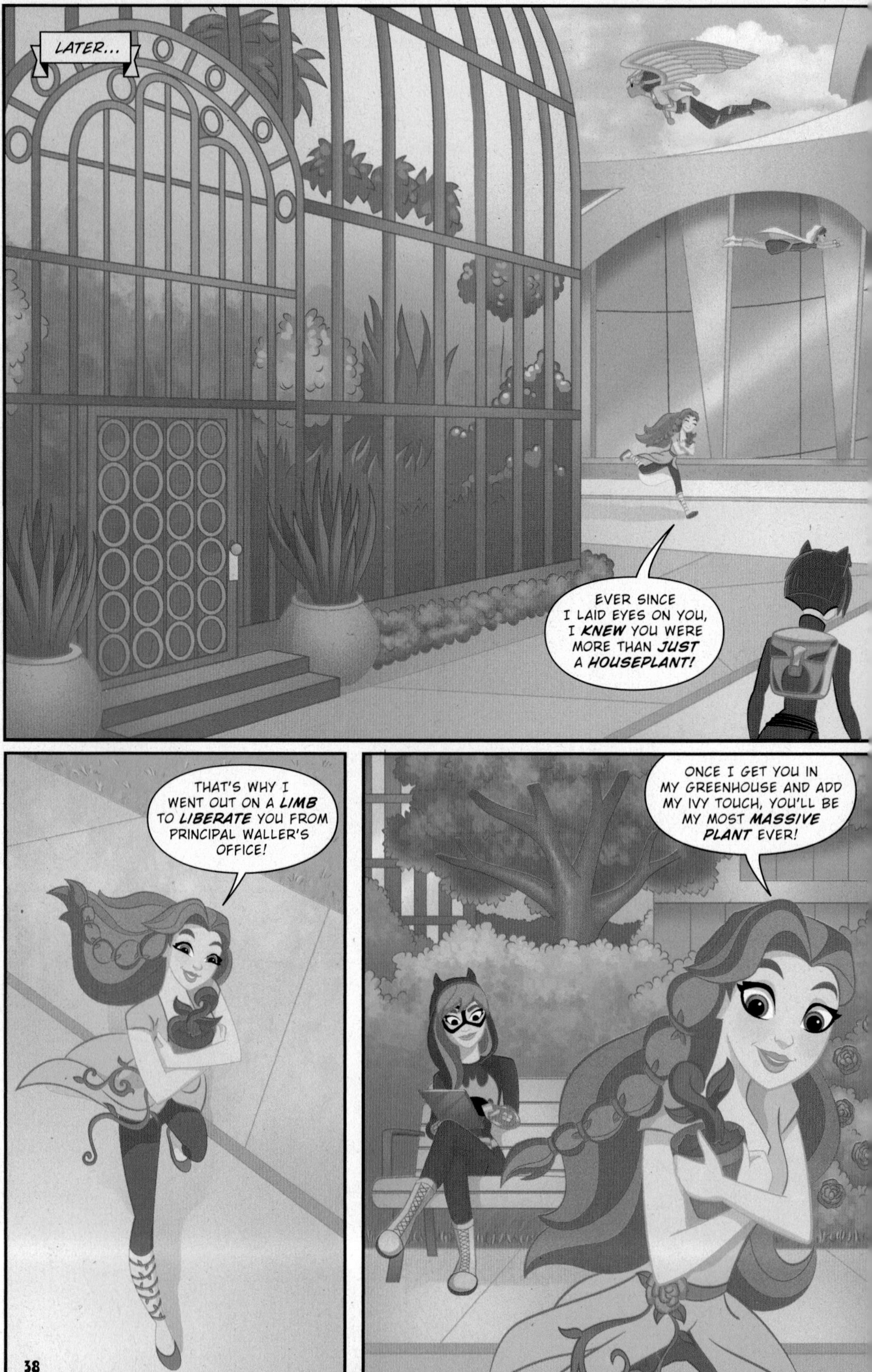
LATER...
EVER SINCE I LAID EYES ON YOU, I KNEW YOU WERE MORE THAN JUST A HOUSEPLANT!
THAT'S WHY I WENT OUT ON A LIMB TO LIBERATE YOU FROM PRINCIPAL WALLER'S OFFICE!
ONCE I GET YOU IN MY GREENHOUSE AND ADD MY IVY TOUCH, YOU'LL BE MY MOST MASSIVE PLANT EVER!

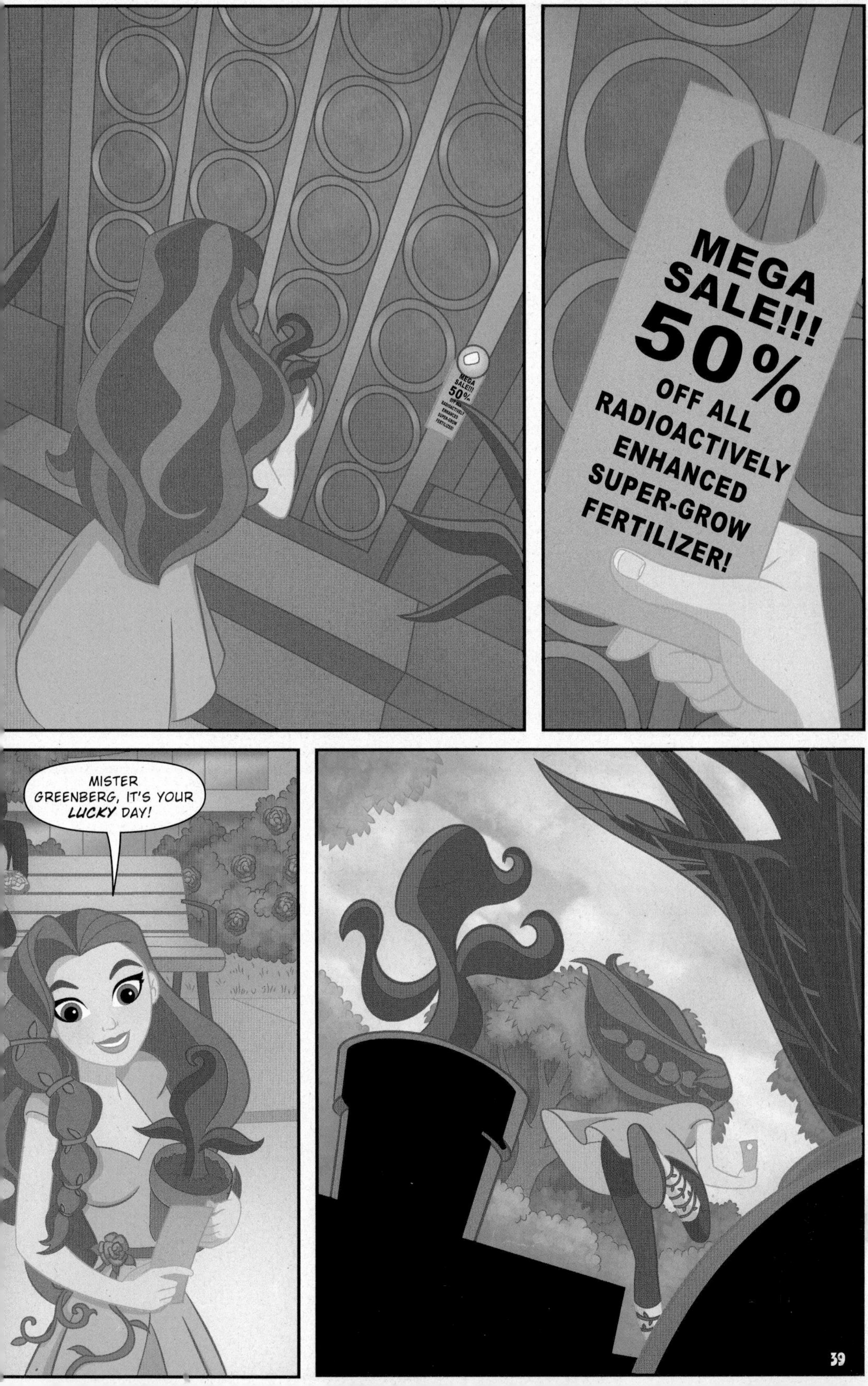

MEGA SALE!!! 50% OFF ALL RADIOACTIVELY ENHANCED SUPER-GROW FERTILIZER!
MEGA SALE!!! 50% OFF ALL RADIOACTIVELY ENHANCED SUPER-GROW FERTILIZER!
MISTER GREENBERG, IT'S YOUR *LUCKY* DAY!

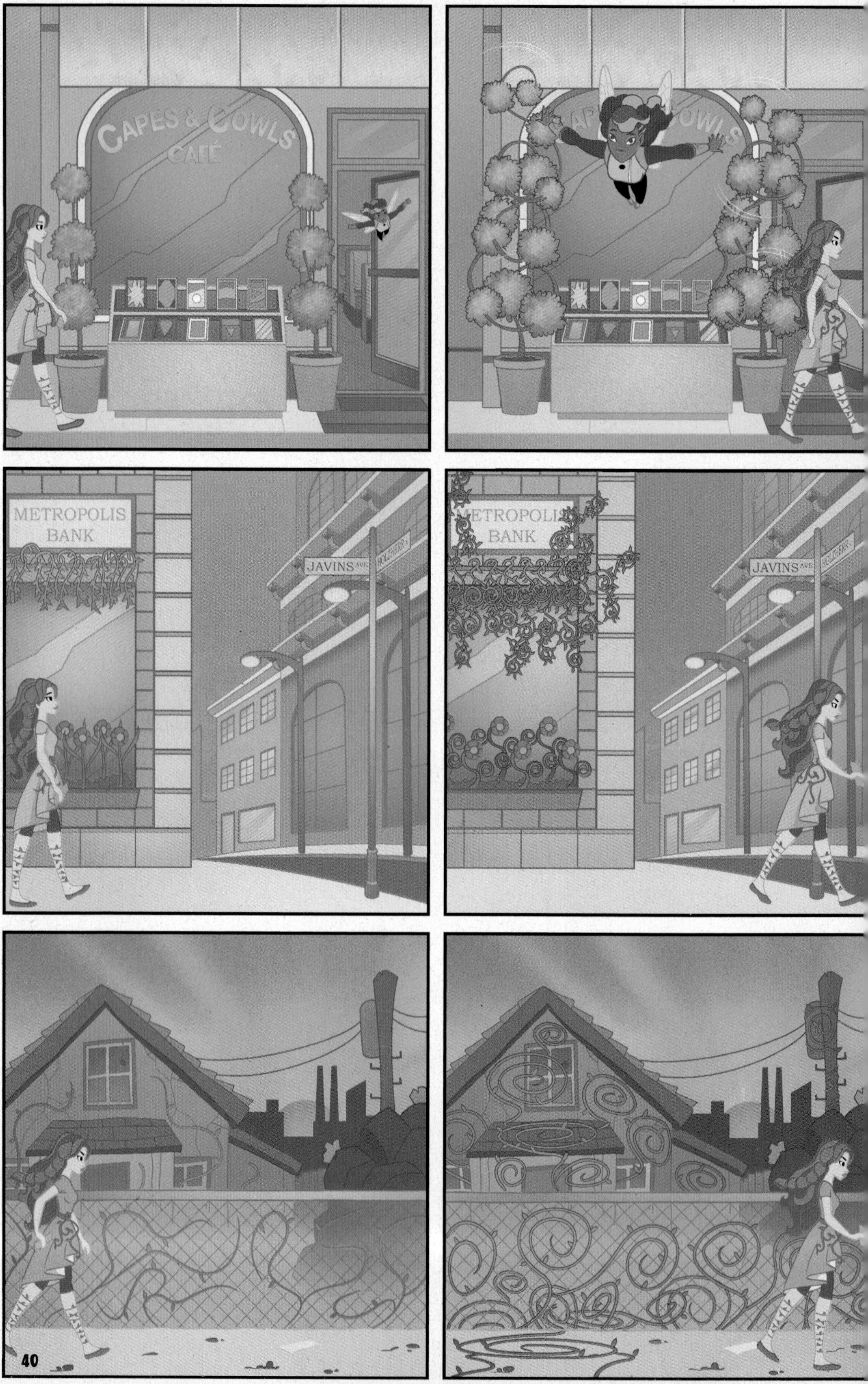
CAPES & COWLS
CAFÉ
METROPOLIS
BANK
JAVINS AVE
METROPOLIS
BANK
JAVINS AVE

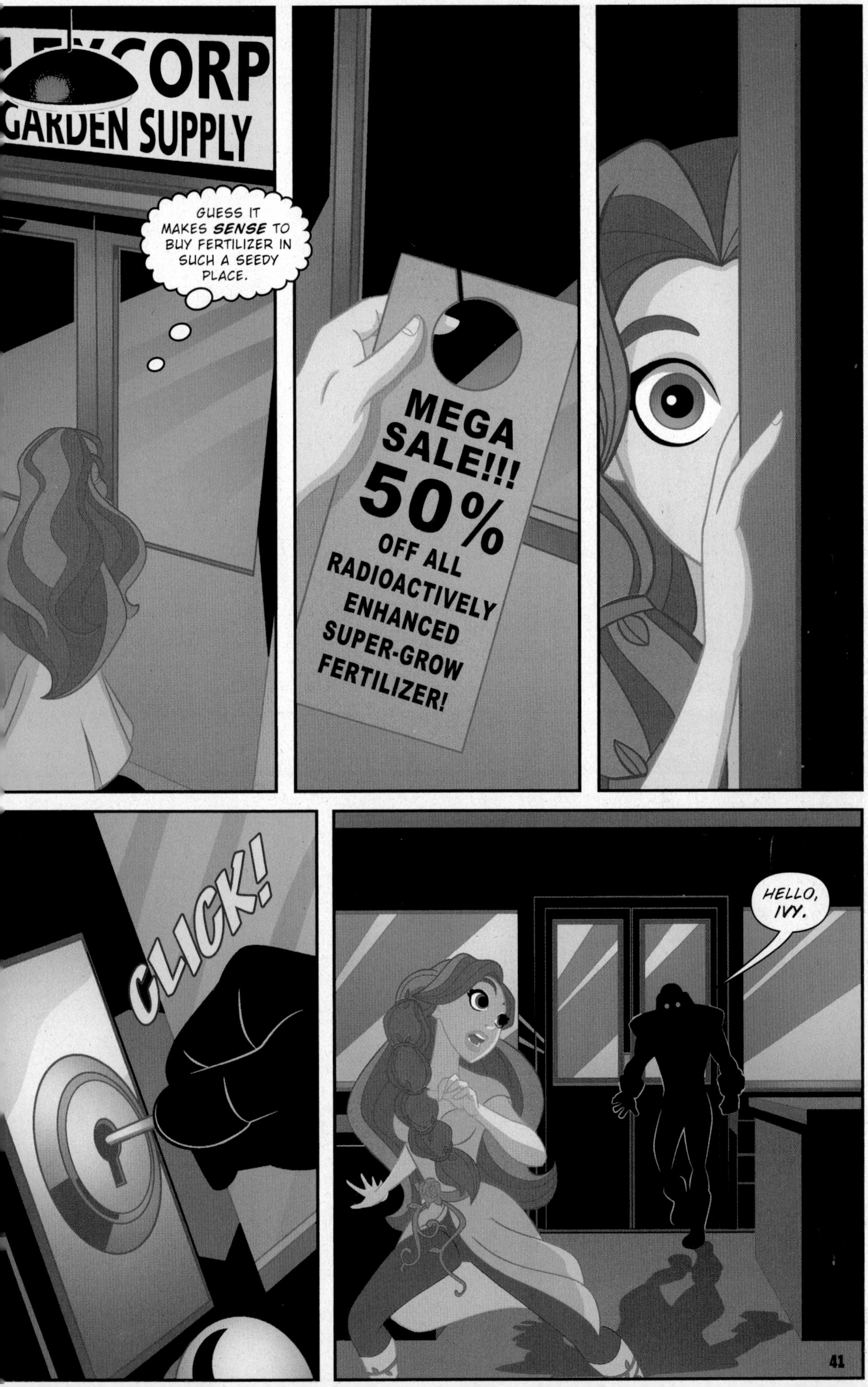

GARDEN SUPPLY
GUESS IT MAKES SENSE TO BUY FERTILIZER IN SUCH A SEEDY PLACE.
MEGA SALE!!! 50% OFF ALL RADIOACTIVELY ENHANCED SUPER-GROW FERTILIZER!
CLICK!
HELLO, IVY.

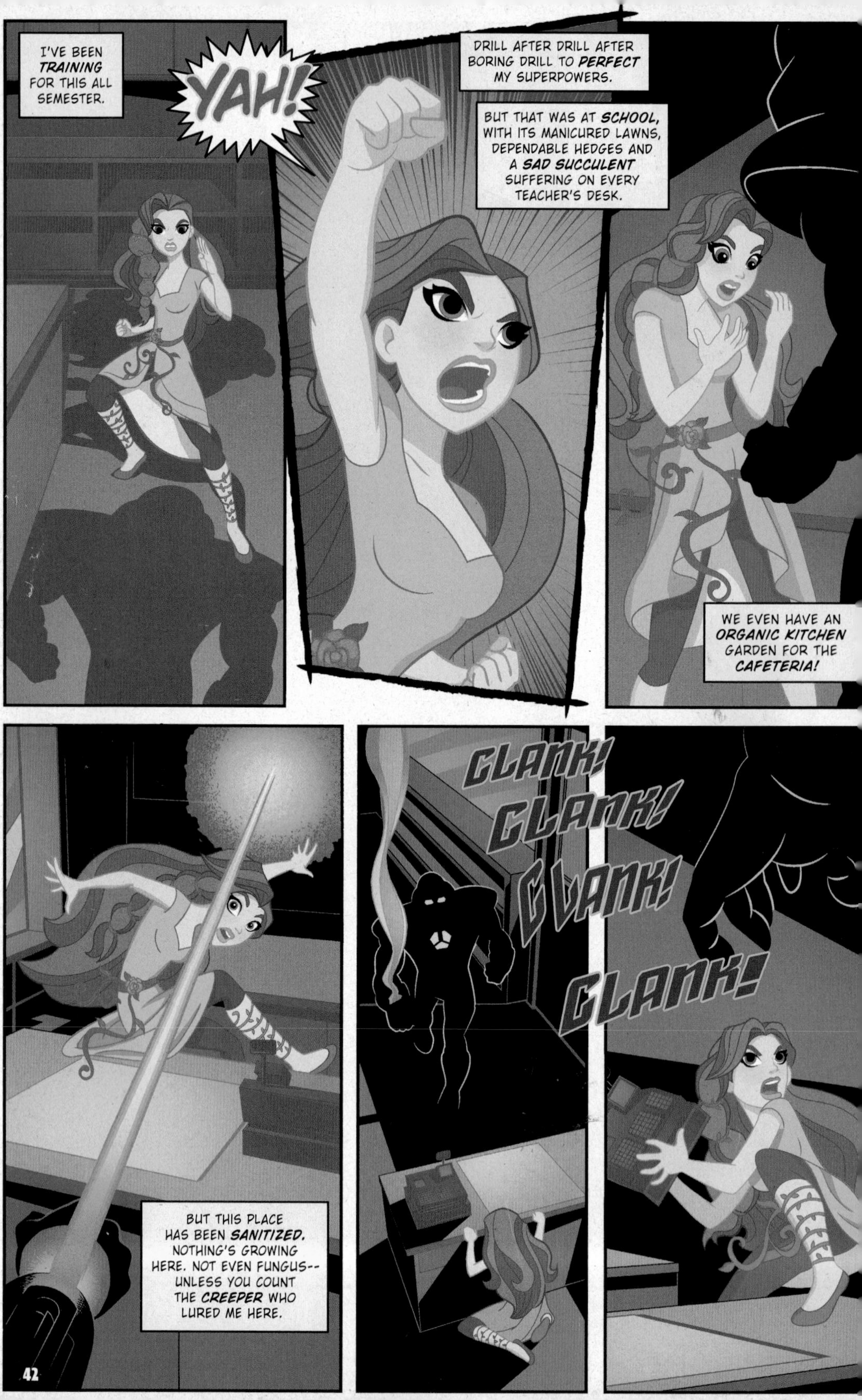
I'VE BEEN TRAINING FOR THIS ALL SEMESTER.
YAH!
DRILL AFTER DRILL AFTER BORING DRILL TO PERFECT MY SUPERPOWERS.
BUT THAT WAS AT SCHOOL, WITH ITS MANICURED LAWNS, DEPENDABLE HEDGES AND A SAD SUCCULENT SUFFERING ON EVERY TEACHER'S DESK.
WE EVEN HAVE AN ORGANIC KITCHEN GARDEN FOR THE CAFETERIA!
BUT THIS PLACE HAS BEEN SANITIZED. NOTHING'S GROWING HERE. NOT EVEN FUNGUS--UNLESS YOU COUNT THE CREEPER WHO LURED ME HERE.
CLANK!
CLANK!
CLANK!
CLANK!

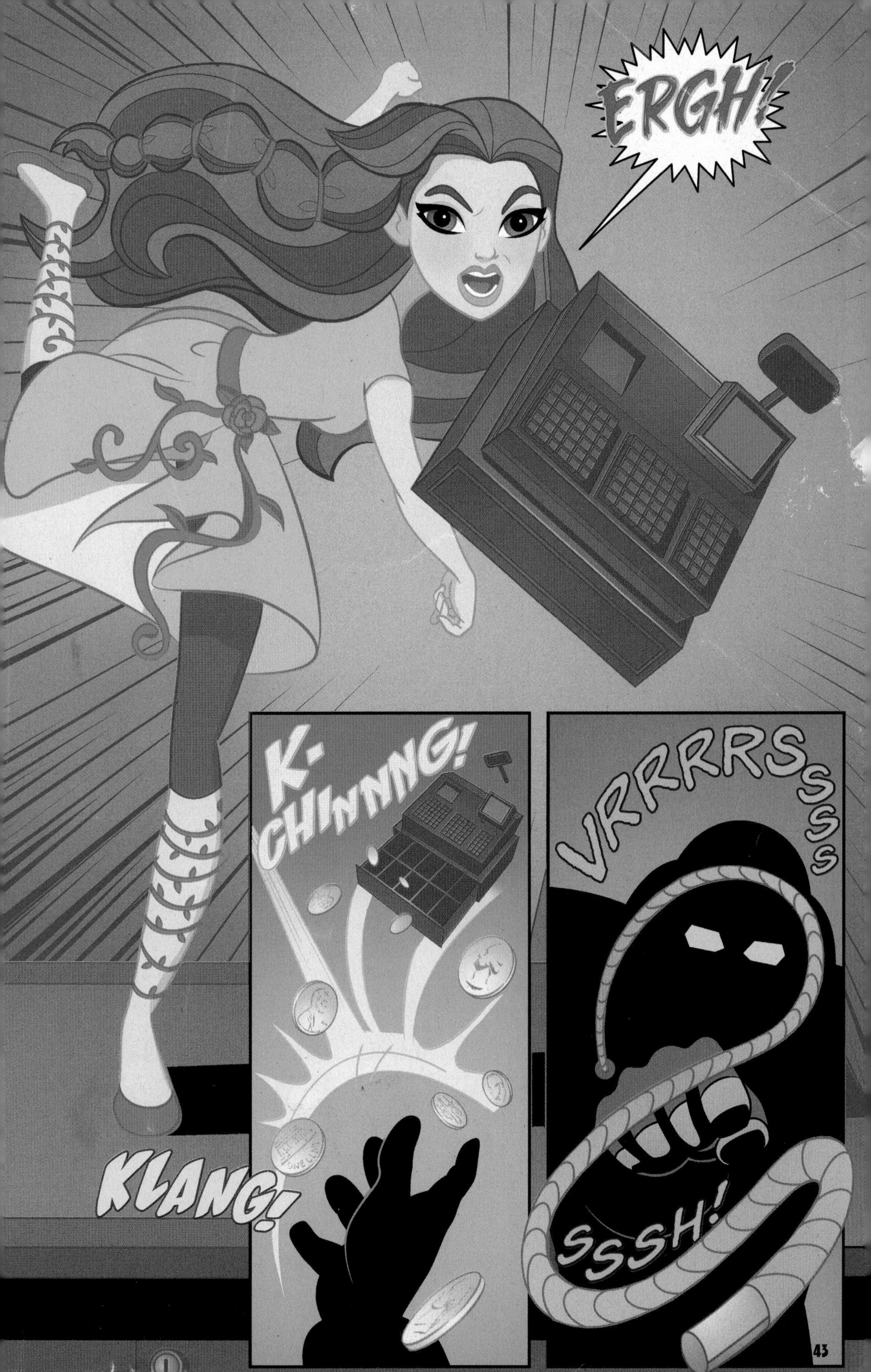
ERGH!
KLANG!
K-CHINNNG!
VRRRRSSSSS
SSSH!

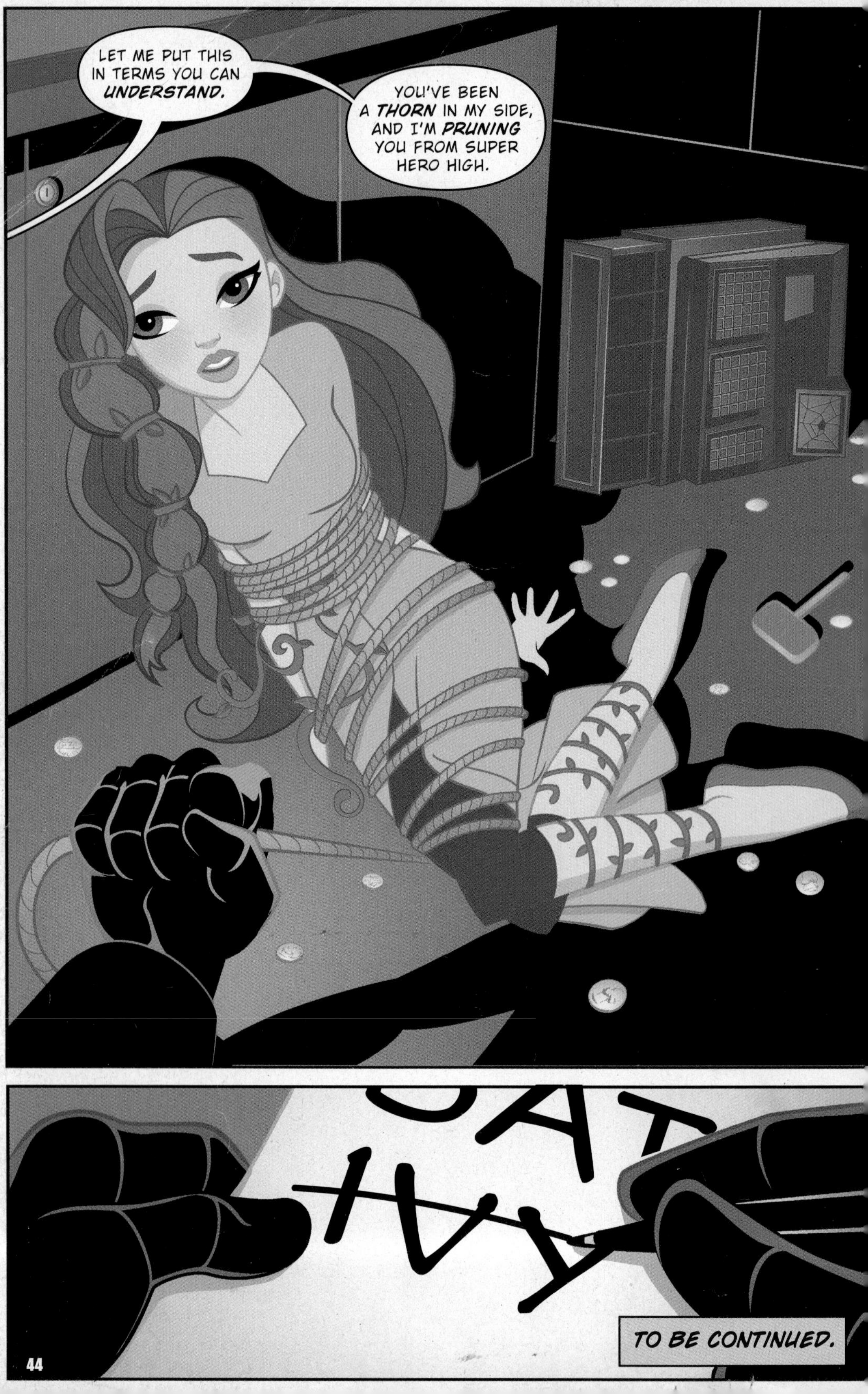
LET ME PUT THIS IN TERMS YOU CAN ***UNDERSTAND.***
YOU'VE BEEN A ***THORN*** IN MY SIDE, AND I'M ***PRUNING*** YOU FROM SUPER HERO HIGH.
TO BE CONTINUED.

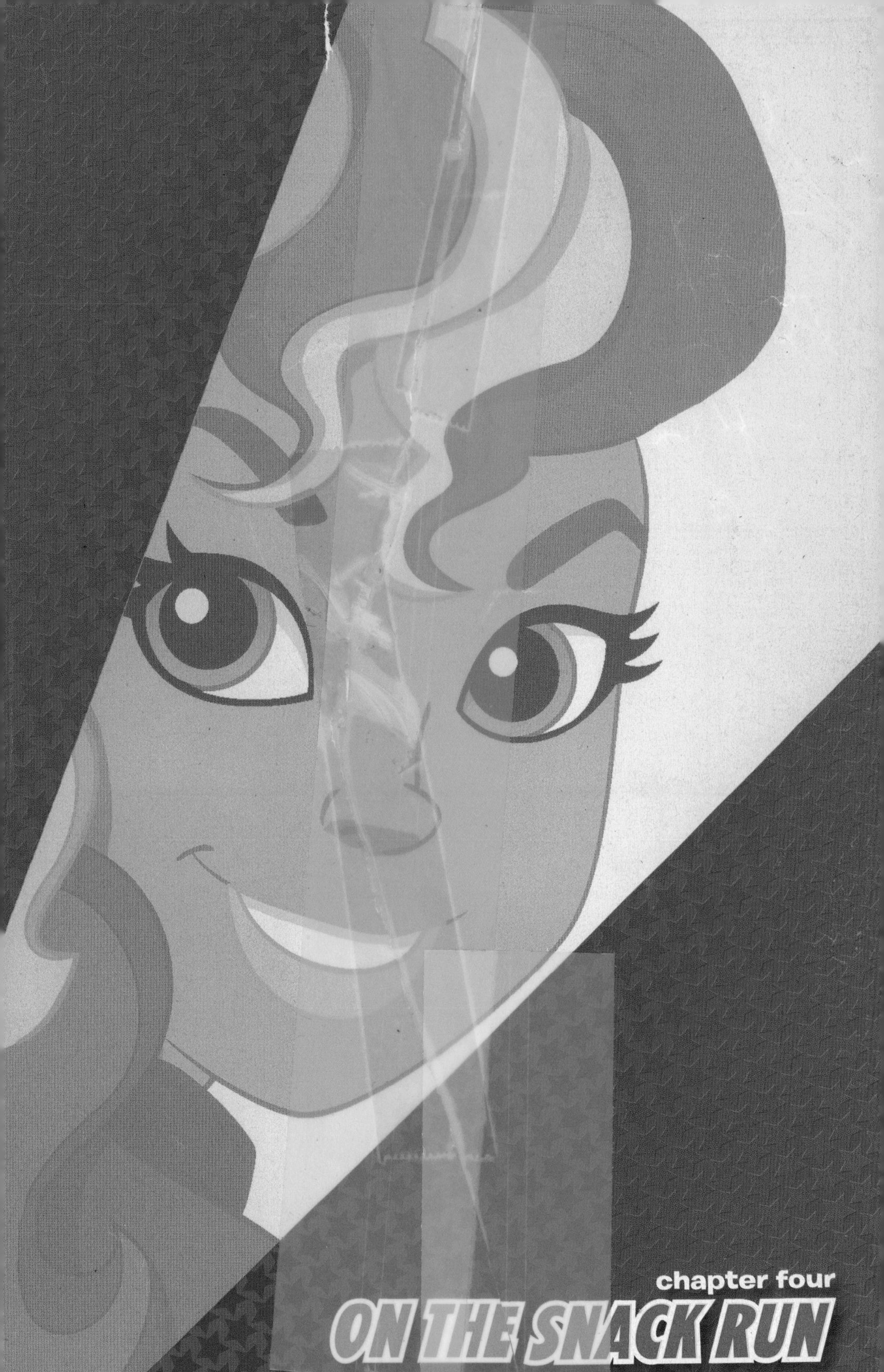

chapter four

ON THE SNACK RUN

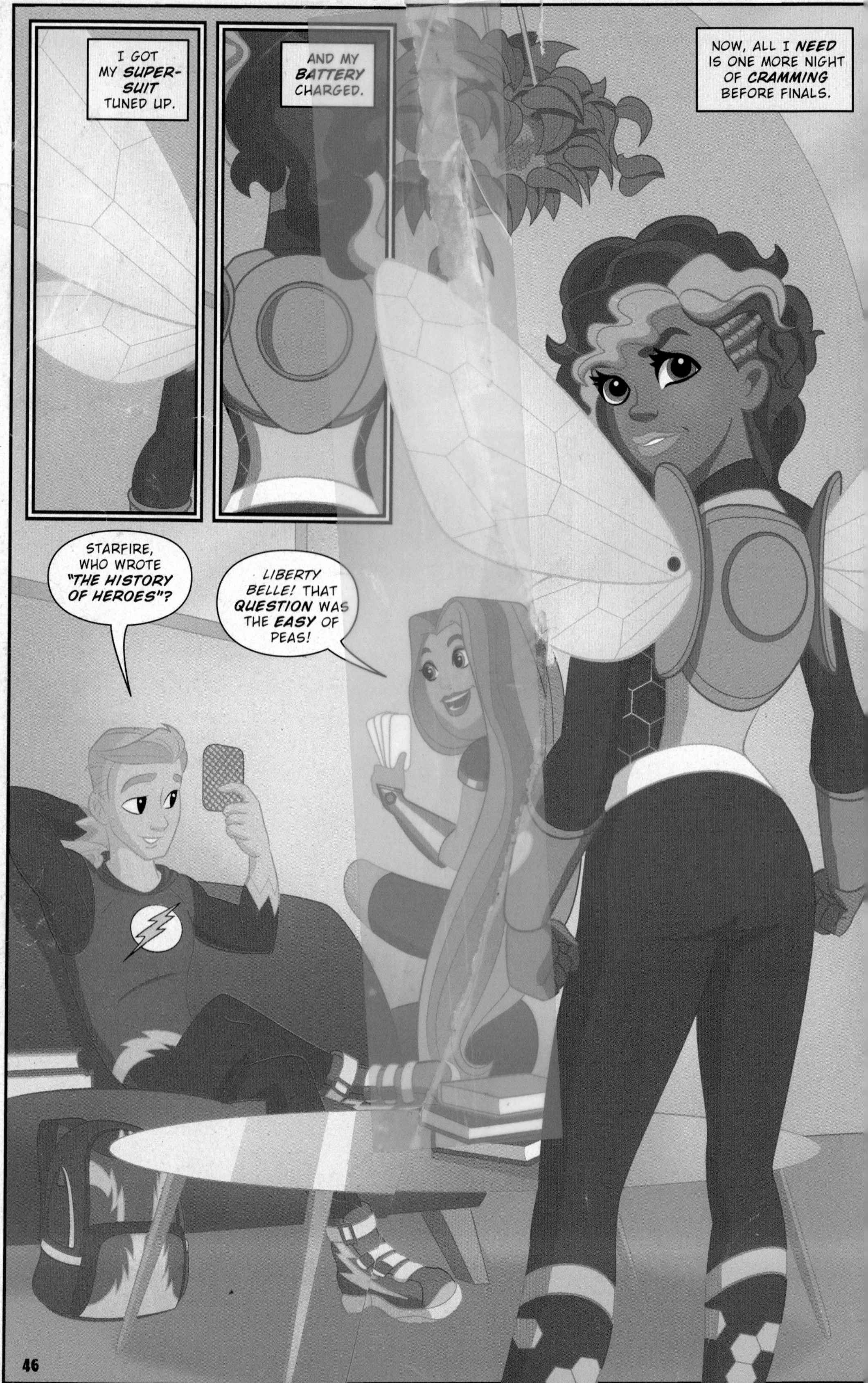
I GOT MY SUPER-SUIT TUNED UP.
AND MY BATTERY CHARGED.
NOW, ALL I NEED IS ONE MORE NIGHT OF CRAMMING BEFORE FINALS.
STARFIRE, WHO WROTE "THE HISTORY OF HEROES"?
LIBERTY BELLE! THAT QUESTION WAS THE EASY OF PEAS!

BUMBLEBEE, NAME THE THREE POWS.

SUPER**POWER**, BRAIN**POWER** AND... UM...ER...

GRRRRRR**RRRR**!

WHAT WAS **THAT**?

COULD IT **BE** THE MAN OF THE BOOGEY!?

WELL, ALL I NEED IS ONE MORE NIGHT OF CRAMMING AND A **HONEY SMOOTHIE**!

IT'S JUST MY **TUMMY**!

THERE IS A **BOOGEY** IN YOUR STOMACH?

NO, I'M **HUNGRY**! CAN'T STUDY FOR FINALS ON AN **EMPTY STOMACH**.

BUT WE HAVE **765** MORE FLASHCARDS TO **GET** THROUGH!

DON'T WORRY, FLASH. I'M GONNA **GRAB** SOME GRUB FROM CAPES & COWLS CAFÉ, 'AND I'LL **B.R.B.**

47

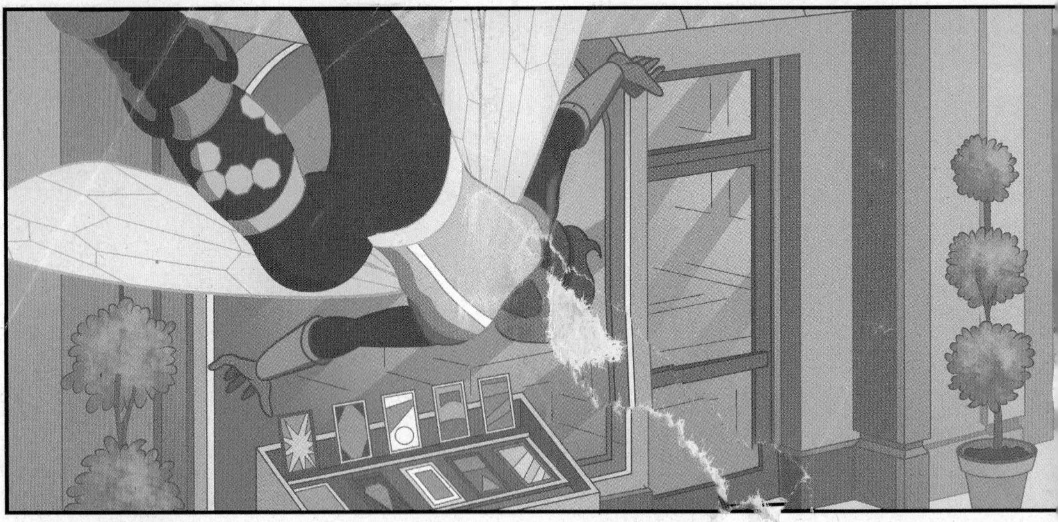

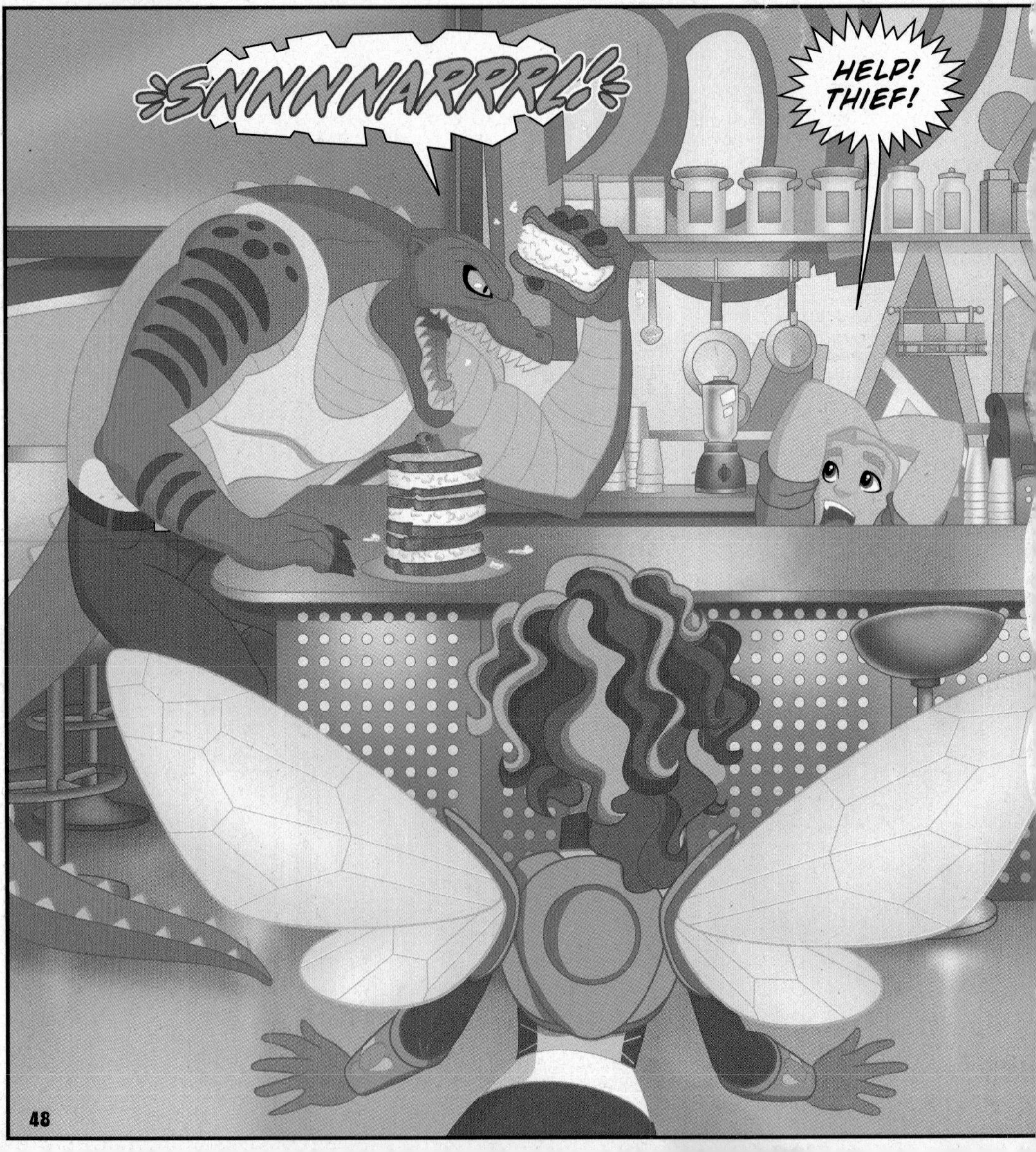
SNNNNARRRRL!
HELP! THIEF!

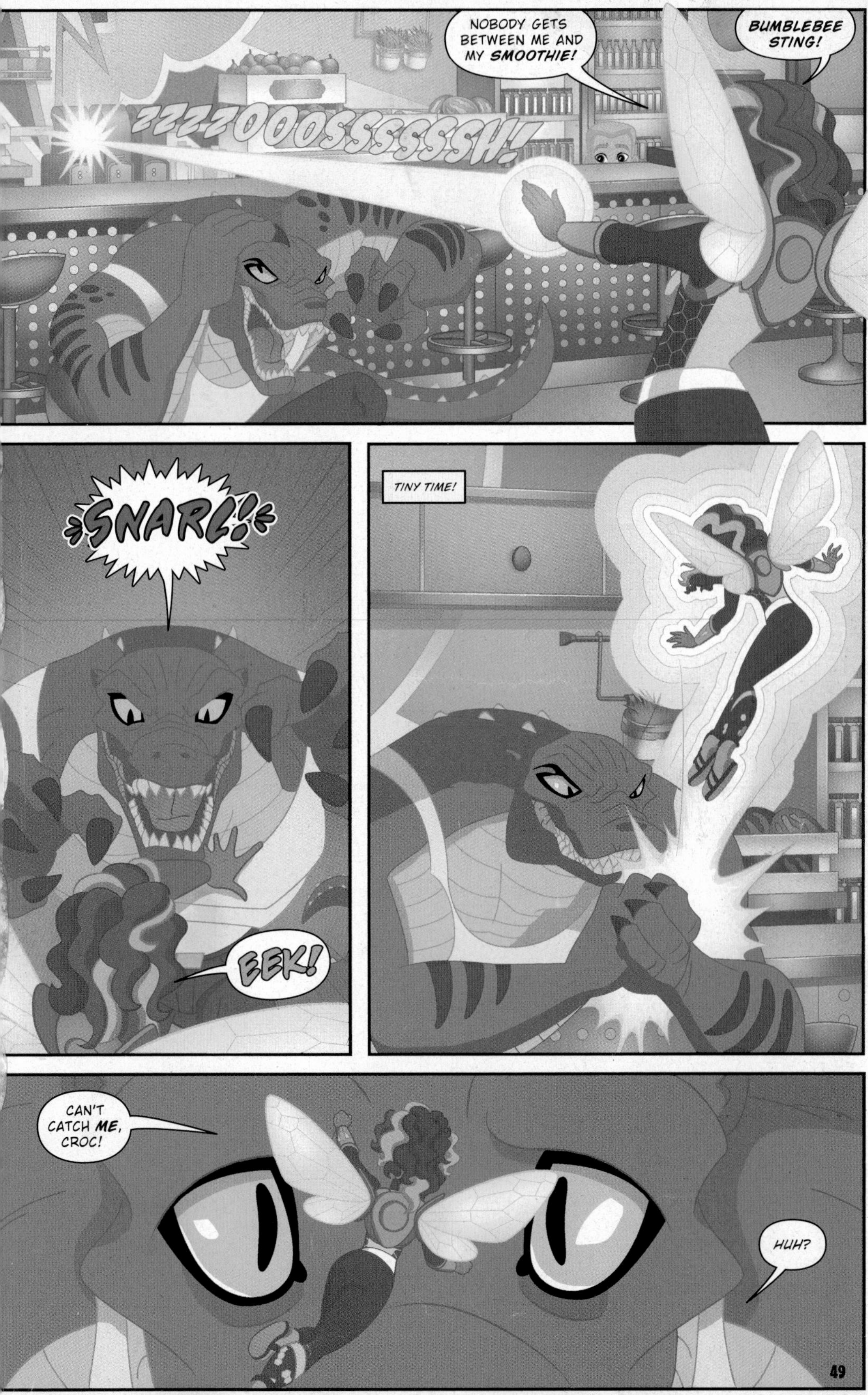

NOBODY GETS BETWEEN ME AND MY SMOOTHIE!
BUMBLEBEE STING!
ZZZZOOOSSSSSSH!
SNARL!
EEK!
TINY TIME!
CAN'T CATCH ME, CROC!
HUH?

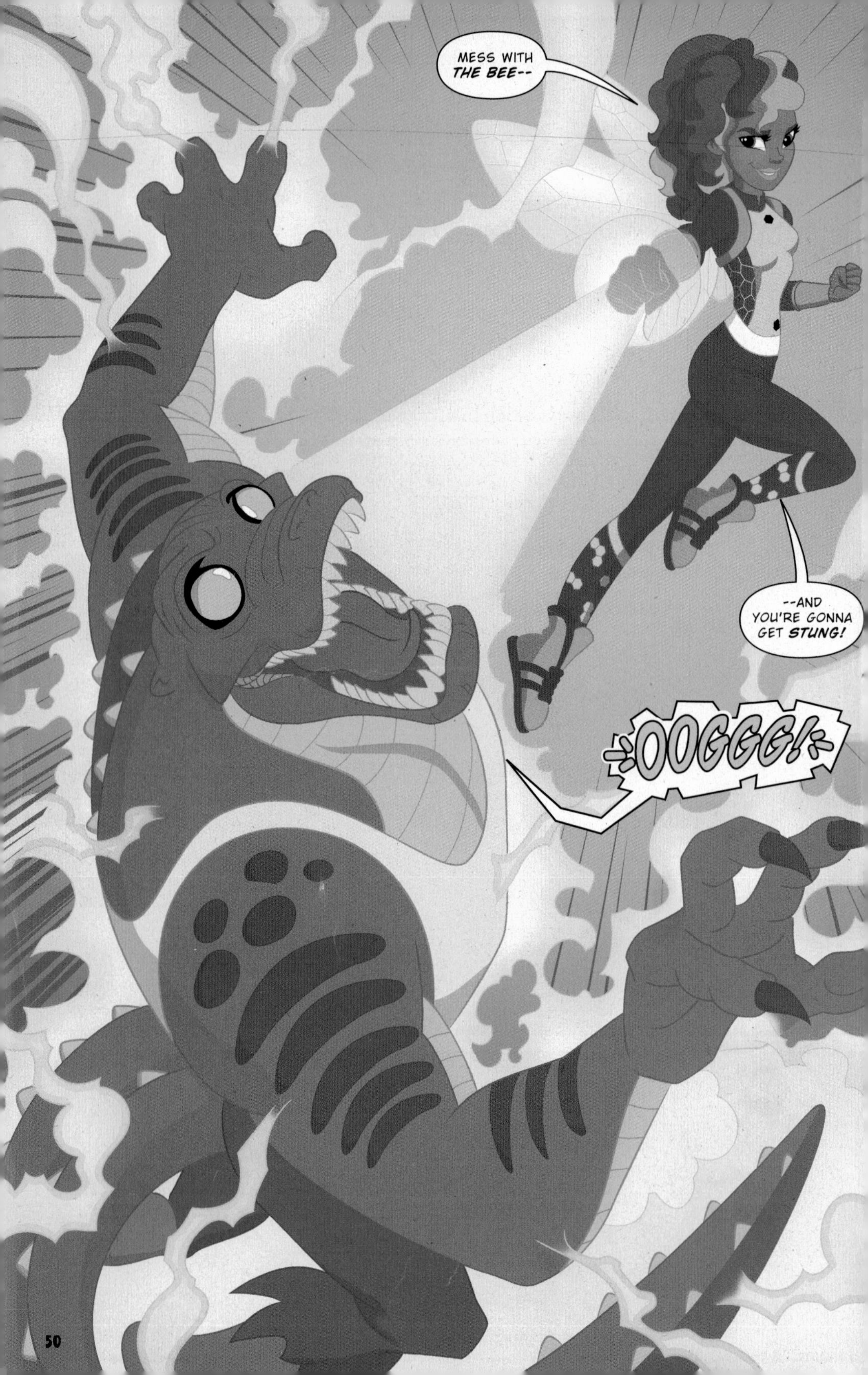
MESS WITH THE BEE--
--AND YOU'RE GONNA GET STUNG!
OOGGG!

*SPECIAL CRIMES UNIT

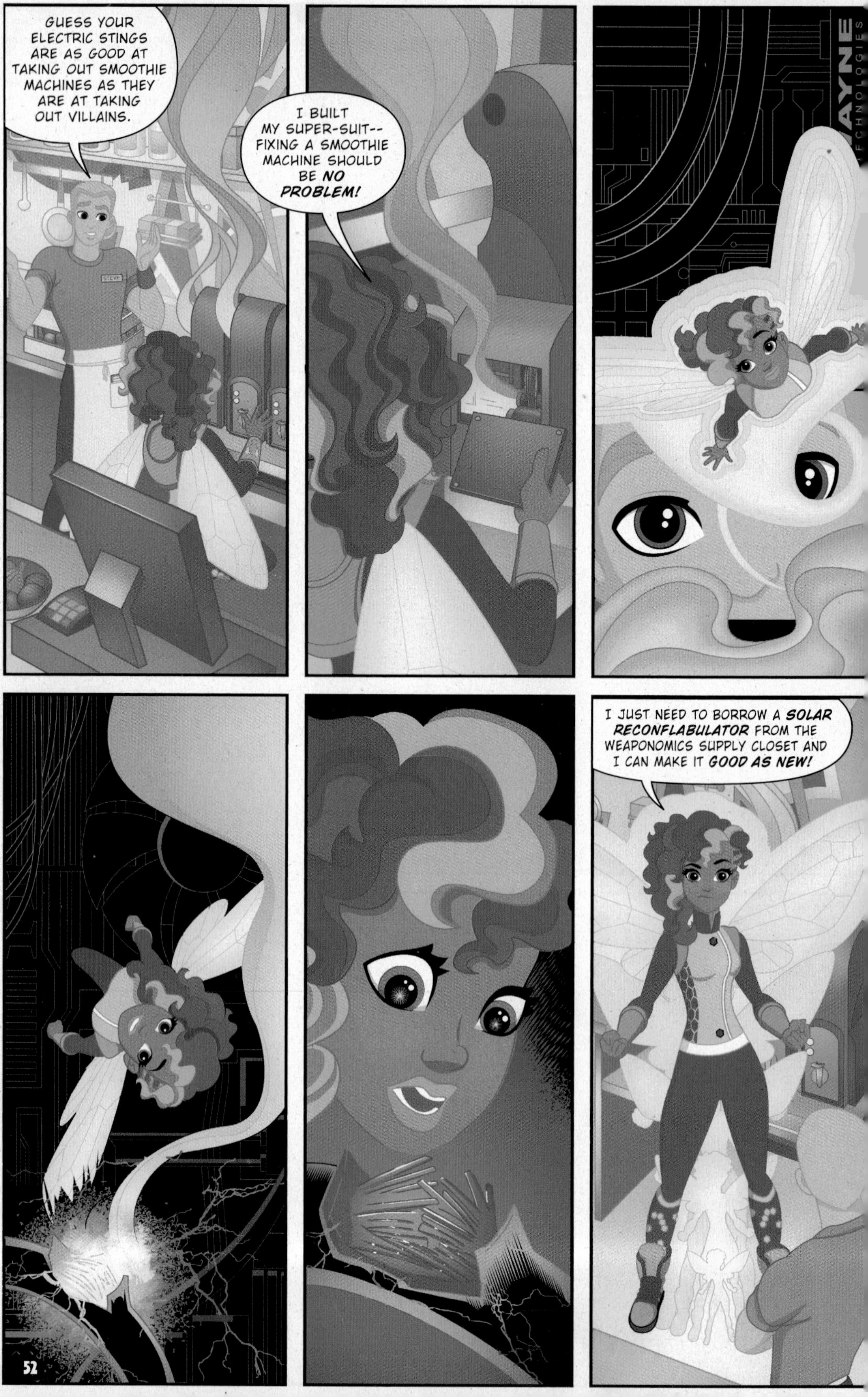
GUESS YOUR ELECTRIC STINGS ARE AS GOOD AT TAKING OUT SMOOTHIE MACHINES AS THEY ARE AT TAKING OUT VILLAINS.
I BUILT MY SUPER-SUIT-- FIXING A SMOOTHIE MACHINE SHOULD BE **NO PROBLEM!**
I JUST NEED TO BORROW A **SOLAR RECONFLABULATOR** FROM THE WEAPONOMICS SUPPLY CLOSET AND I CAN MAKE IT **GOOD AS NEW!**

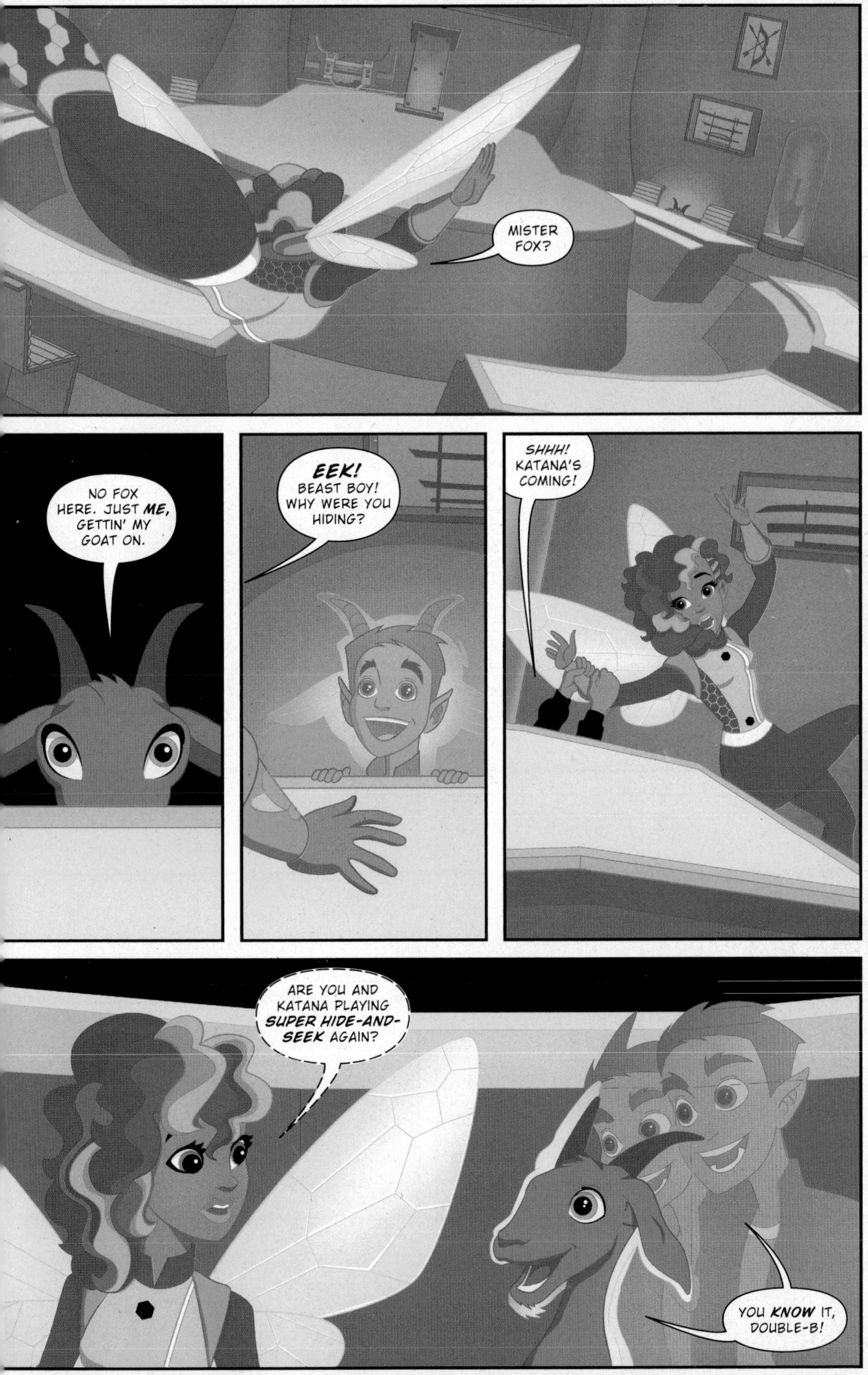

MISTER FOX?
NO FOX HERE. JUST ME, GETTIN' MY GOAT ON.
EEK! BEAST BOY! WHY WERE YOU HIDING?
SHHH! KATANA'S COMING!
ARE YOU AND KATANA PLAYING SUPER HIDE-AND-SEEK AGAIN?
YOU KNOW IT, DOUBLE-B!

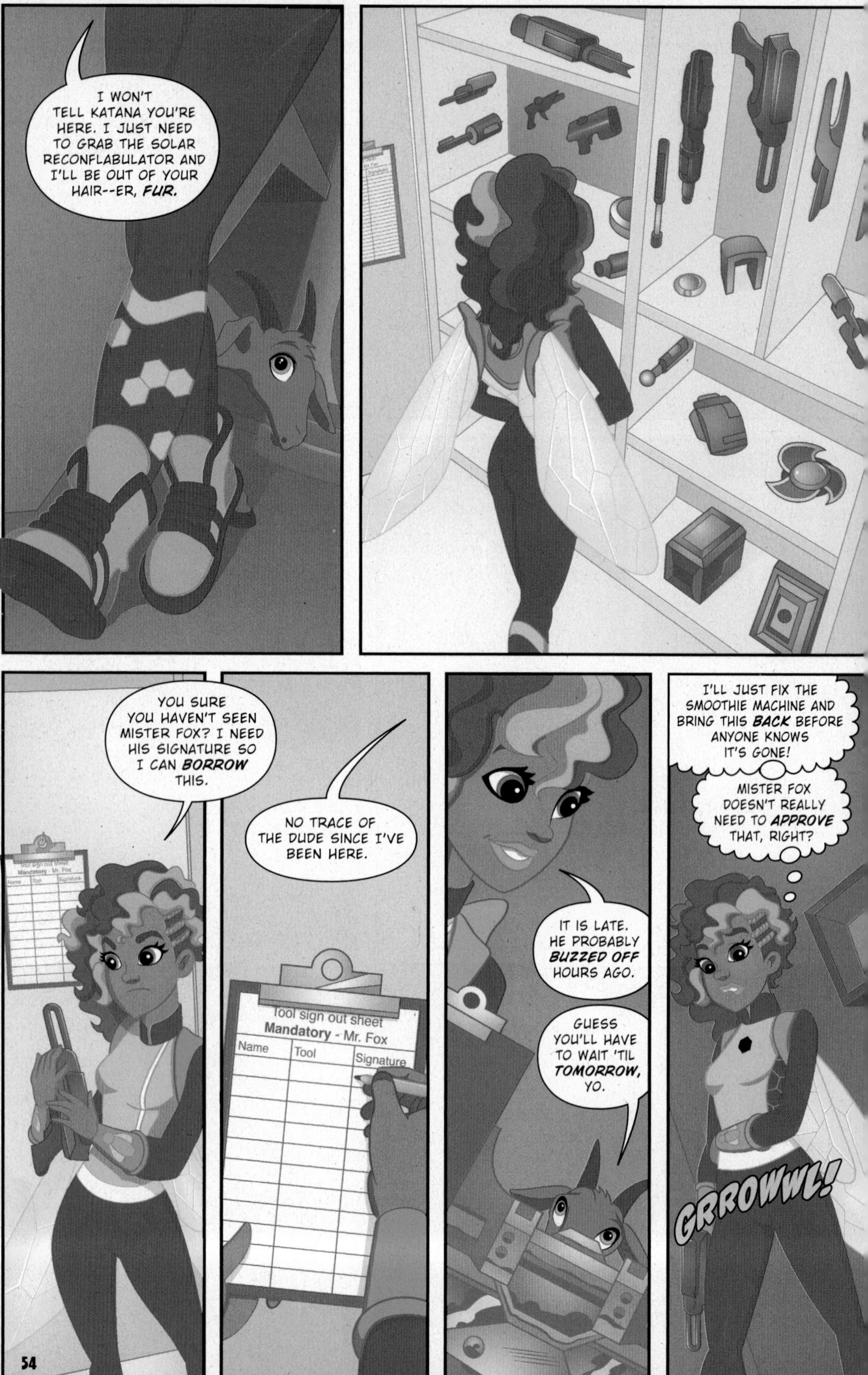
I WON'T TELL KATANA YOU'RE HERE. I JUST NEED TO GRAB THE SOLAR RECONFLABULATOR AND I'LL BE OUT OF YOUR HAIR--ER, FUR.
YOU SURE YOU HAVEN'T SEEN MISTER FOX? I NEED HIS SIGNATURE SO I CAN BORROW THIS.
NO TRACE OF THE DUDE SINCE I'VE BEEN HERE.
Tool sign out sheet
Mandatory - Mr. Fox
Name
Tool
Signature
IT IS LATE. HE PROBABLY BUZZED OFF HOURS AGO.
GUESS YOU'LL HAVE TO WAIT 'TIL TOMORROW, YO.
I'LL JUST FIX THE SMOOTHIE MACHINE AND BRING THIS BACK BEFORE ANYONE KNOWS IT'S GONE!
MISTER FOX DOESN'T REALLY NEED TO APPROVE THAT, RIGHT?
GRROWWL!

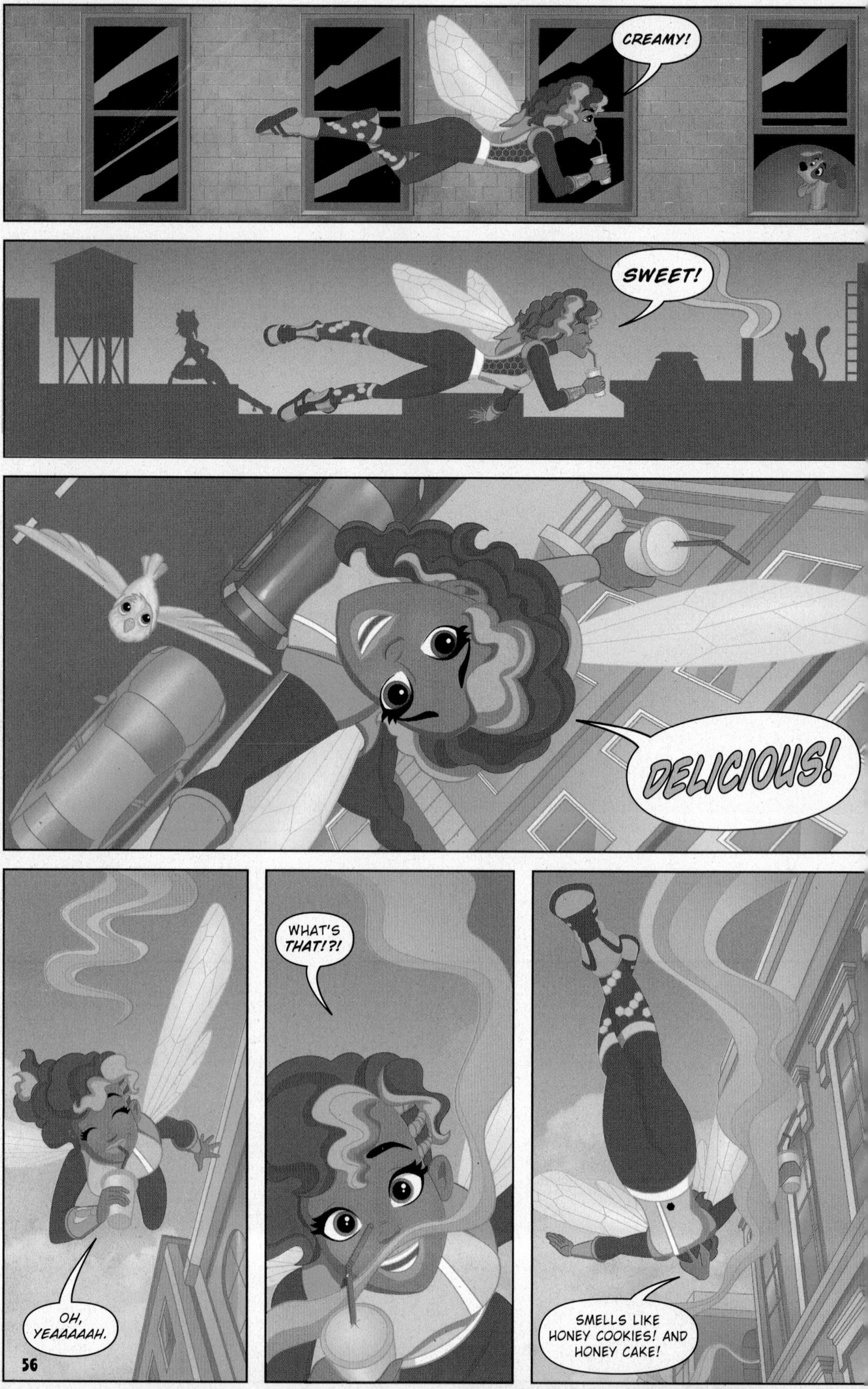
CREAMY!
SWEET!
DELICIOUS!
OH, YEAAAAAH.
WHAT'S THAT!?!
SMELLS LIKE HONEY COOKIES! AND HONEY CAKE!

AND HONEY **LATTES!**

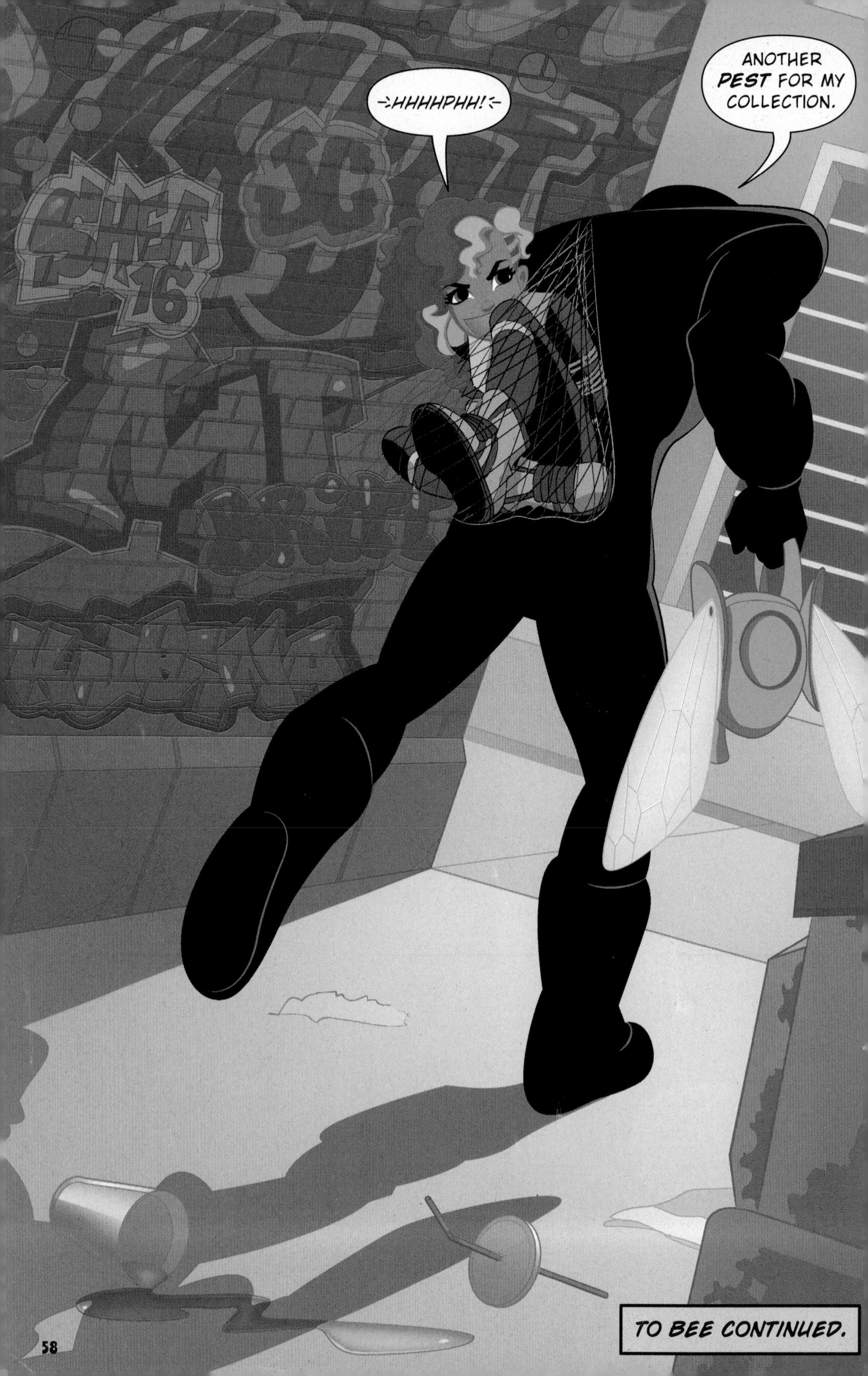
-=HHHHPHH!=-
ANOTHER PEST FOR MY COLLECTION.
TO BEE CONTINUED.

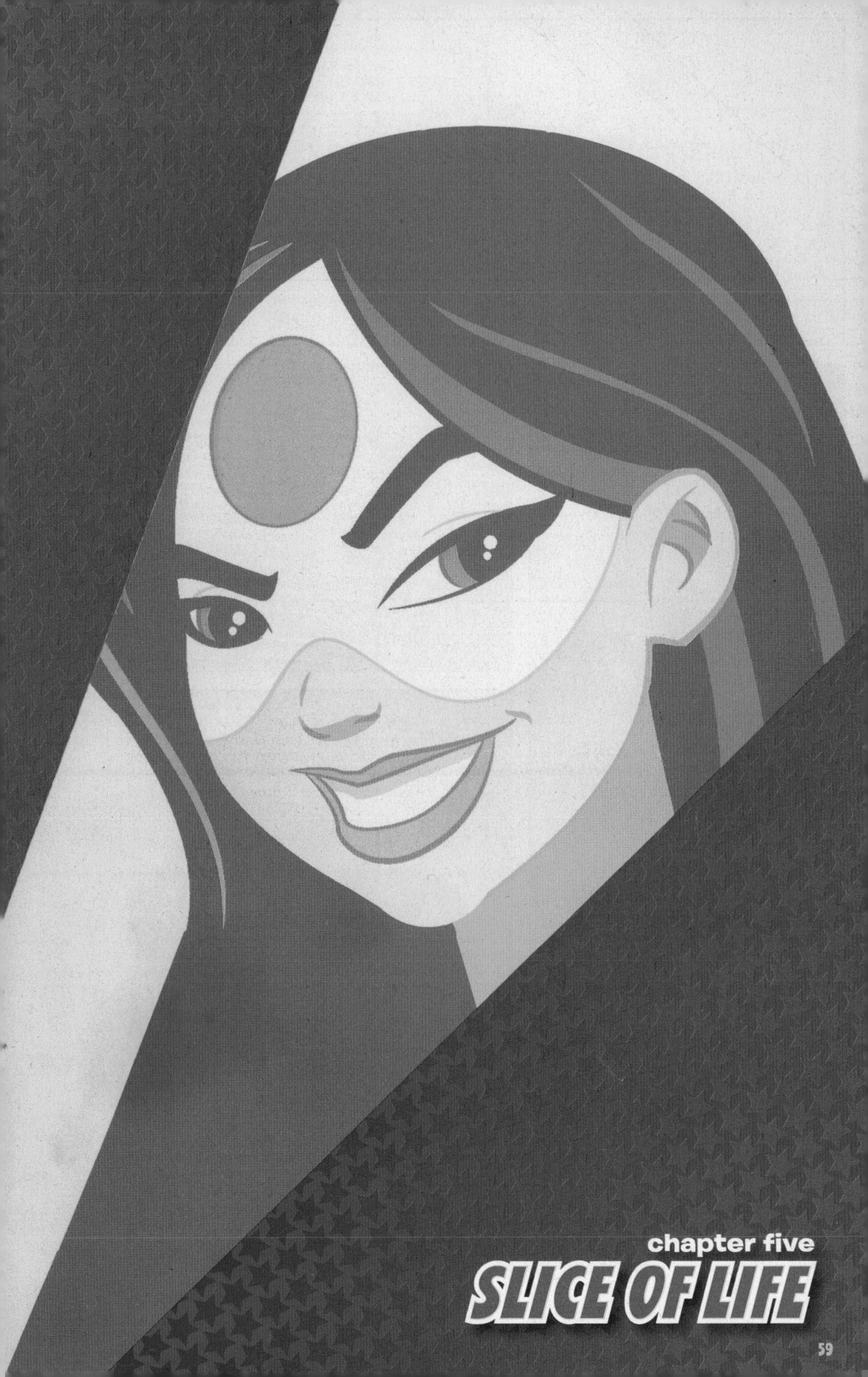

chapter five
SLICE OF LIFE

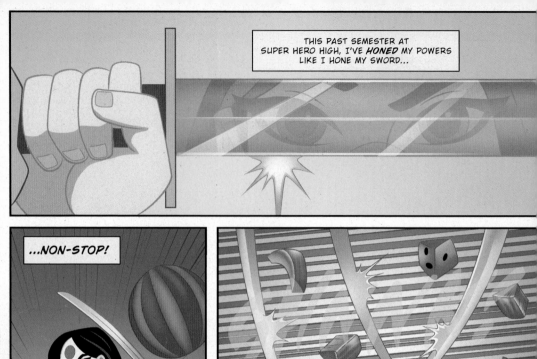

THIS PAST SEMESTER AT SUPER HERO HIGH, I'VE **HONED** MY POWERS LIKE I HONE MY SWORD...

...NON-STOP!

EACH SWING OF MY SWORD MAKES MY MIND AND BODY **SHARPER**, MORE PREPARED TO CUT THROUGH TOMORROW'S FINALS.

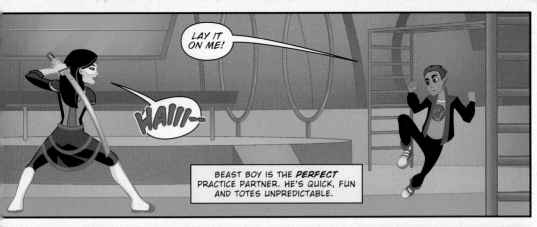

LAY IT ON ME!

HAIII—

BEAST BOY IS THE *PERFECT* PRACTICE PARTNER. HE'S QUICK, FUN AND TOTES UNPREDICTABLE.

WOOOSH!!

--YAH!

ANY WAY YOU SLICE IT, BEAST BOY IS A CUT ABOVE.

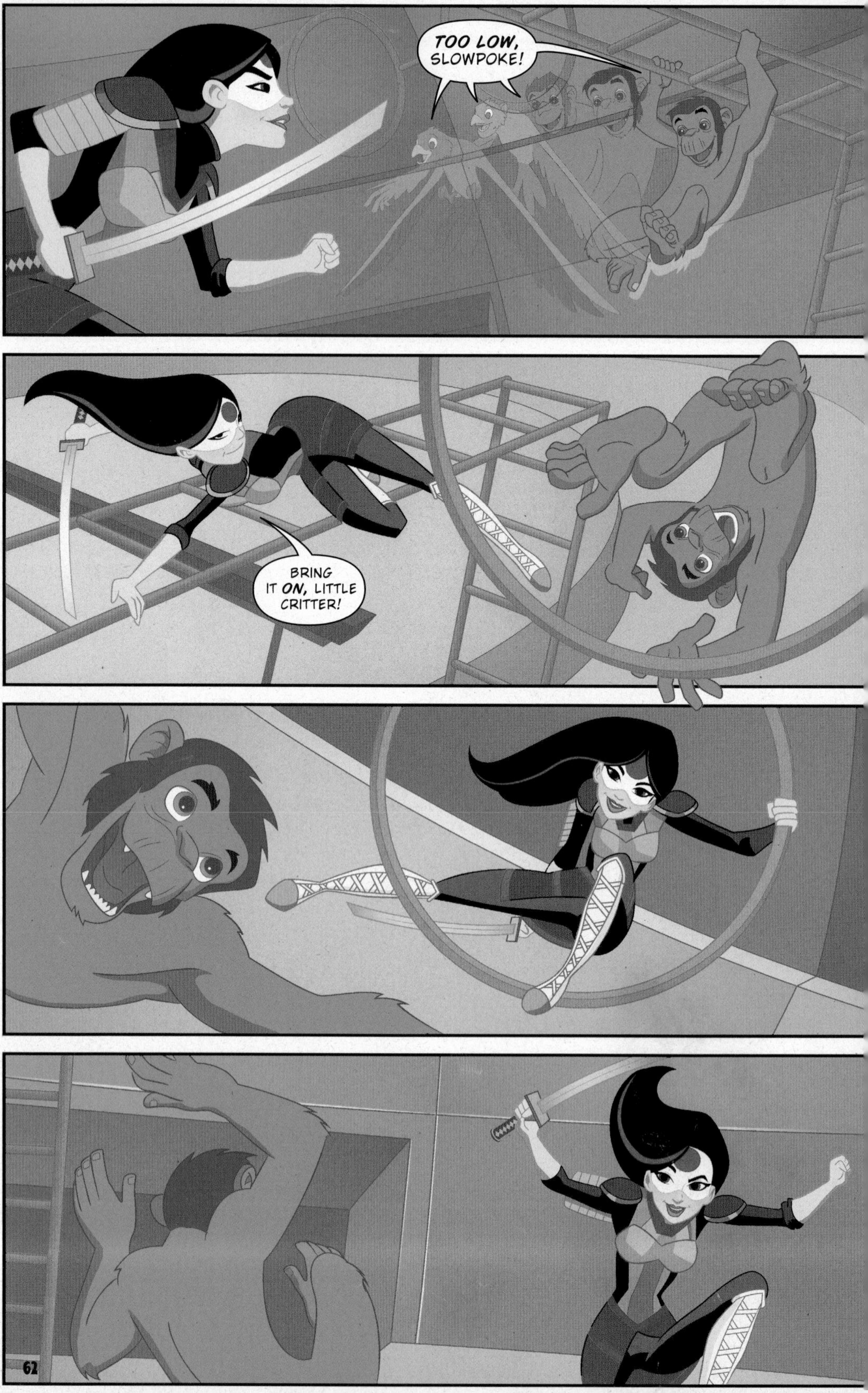
TOO LOW, SLOWPOKE!
BRING IT ON, LITTLE CRITTER!

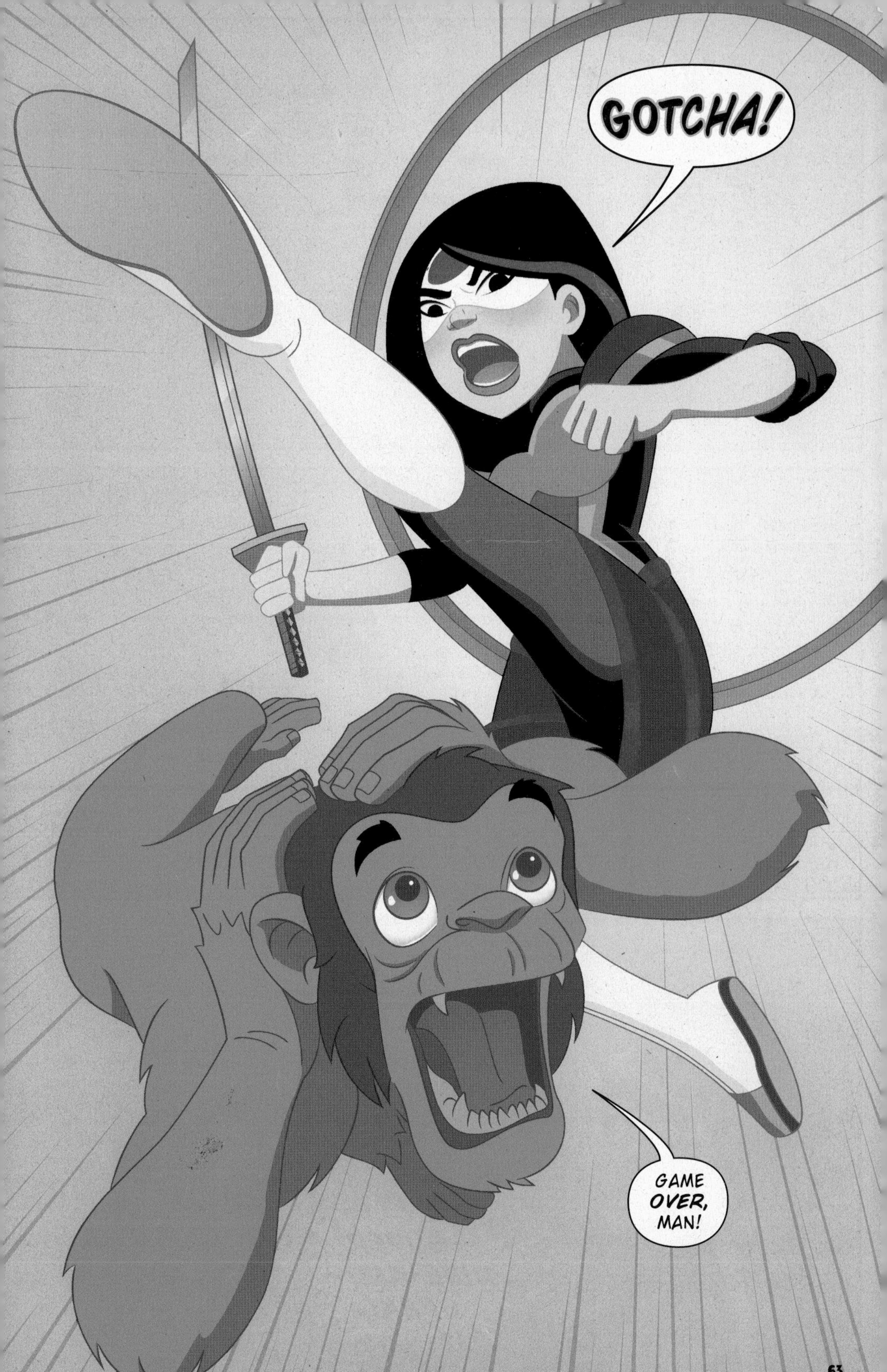
GOTCHA!
GAME OVER, MAN!

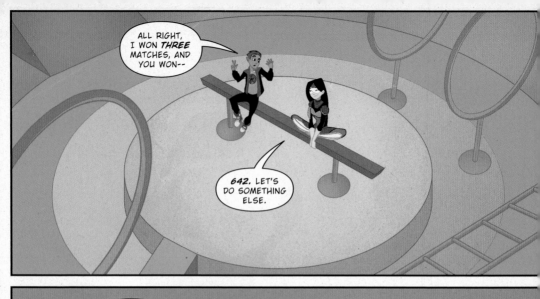

FOUND YOU!

AW, MAN!

TOO EASY!

ZINNNG!

GOTCHA AGAIN!

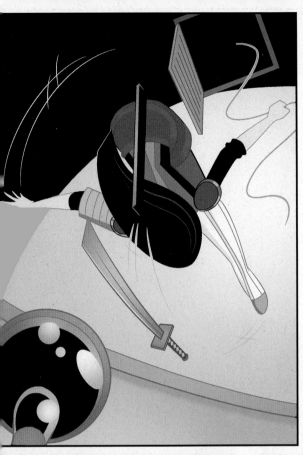

AHH! POINTY!

SH-I-N-G!

PRINCIPAL WALLER'S GONNA GIVE US A DETENTION *LIFE* SENTENCE! WHAT ARE WE GONNA DO?

WE HAVE TO *FIX* IT!

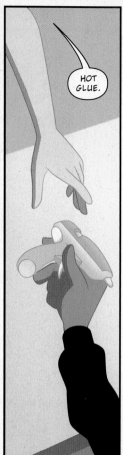

HOT GLUE.

LOOKS **GOOD** TO THESE HAWK EYES!

LET'S GET IT BACK TO THE PRINCIPAL'S OFFICE.

WE'VE GOT WALLER TO THE LEFT.

BEAST BOY, YOU DISTRACT PRINCIPAL WALLER. **I'LL** REPLACE THE TROPHY.

YOU **GOT** IT, BOSS LADY!

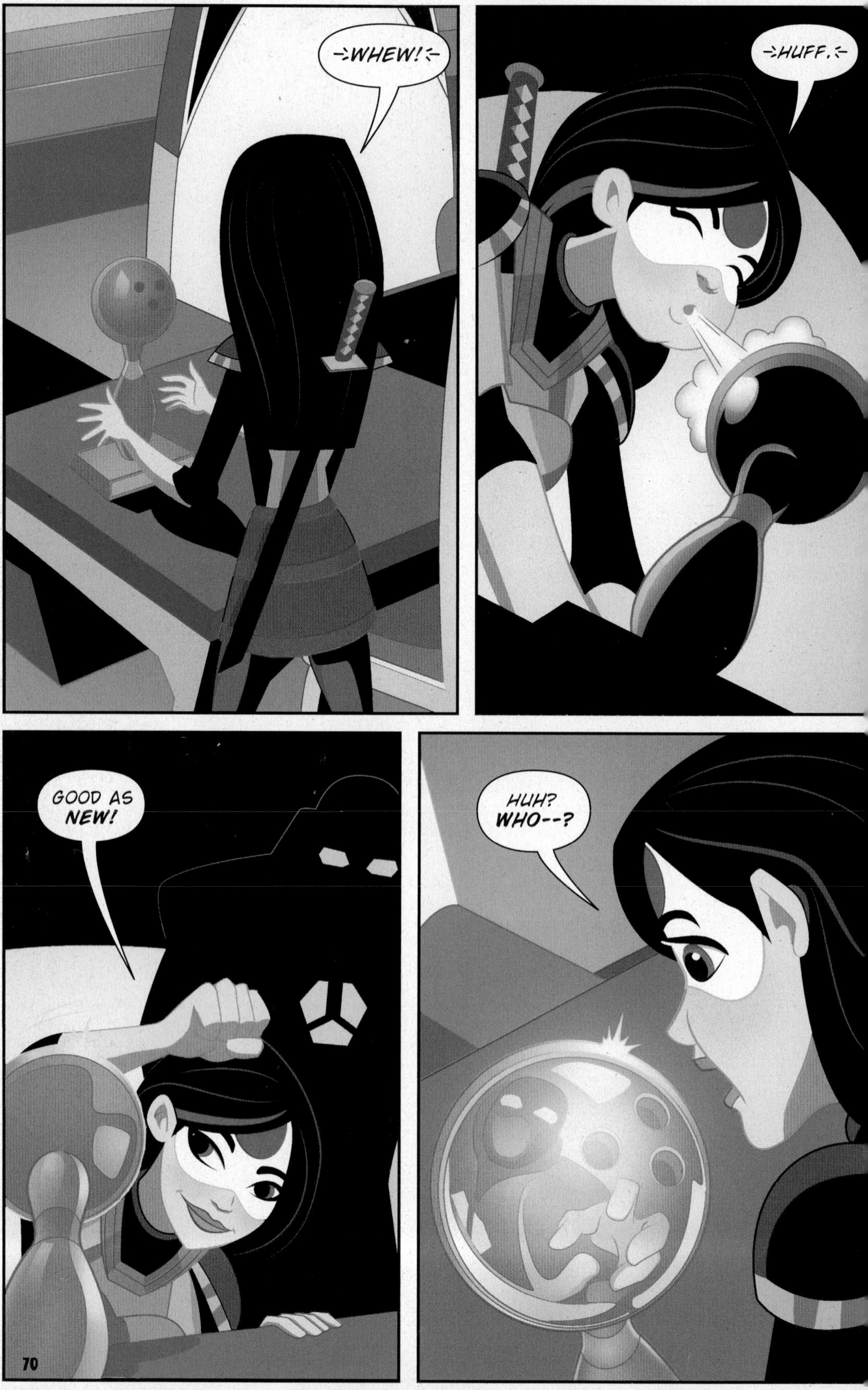
WHEW!
HUFF.
GOOD AS NEW!
HUH? WHO--?

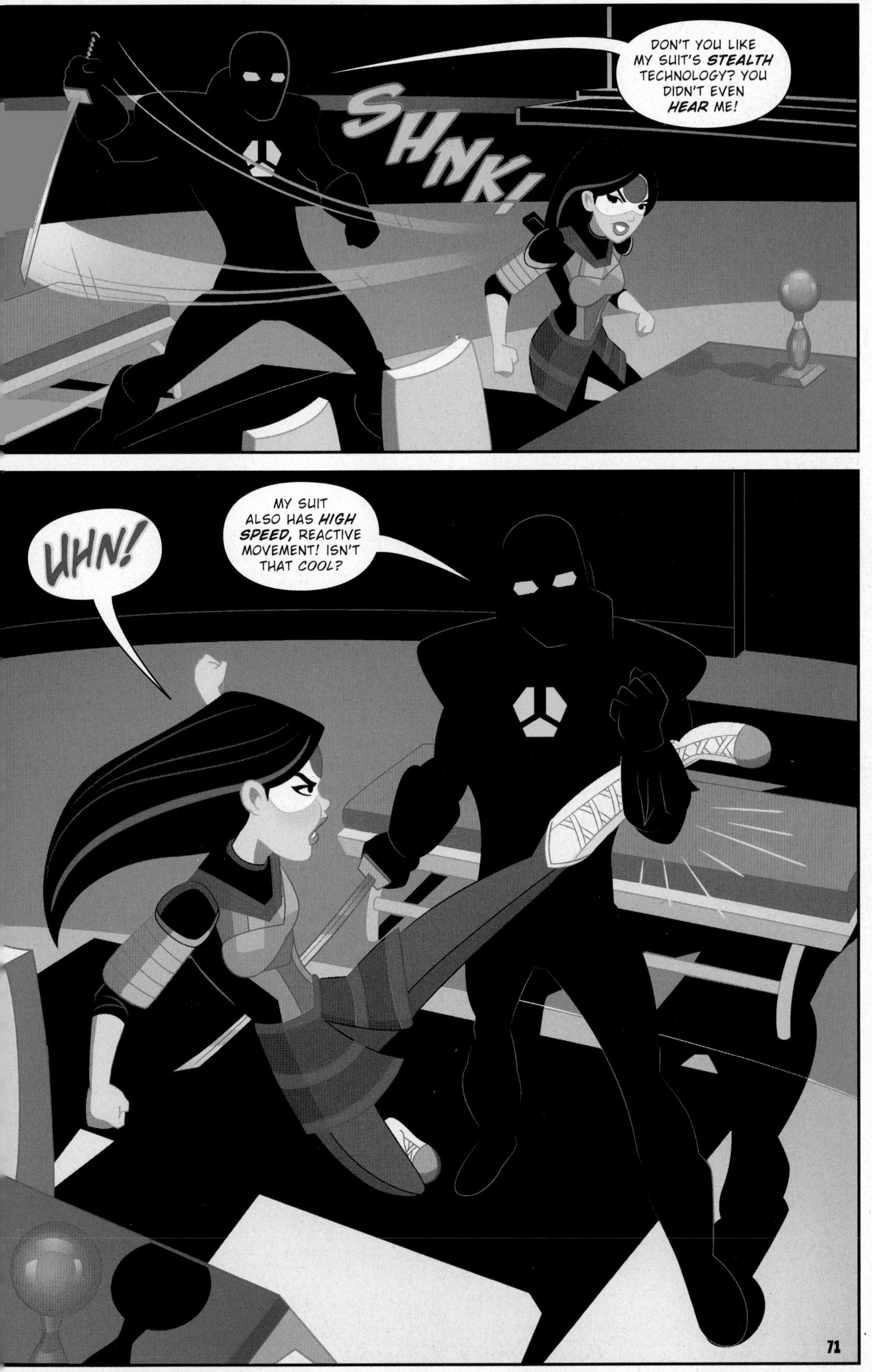
DON'T YOU LIKE MY SUIT'S **STEALTH** TECHNOLOGY? YOU DIDN'T EVEN **HEAR** ME!
SHNK!
UHN!
MY SUIT ALSO HAS **HIGH SPEED,** REACTIVE MOVEMENT! ISN'T THAT *COOL*?

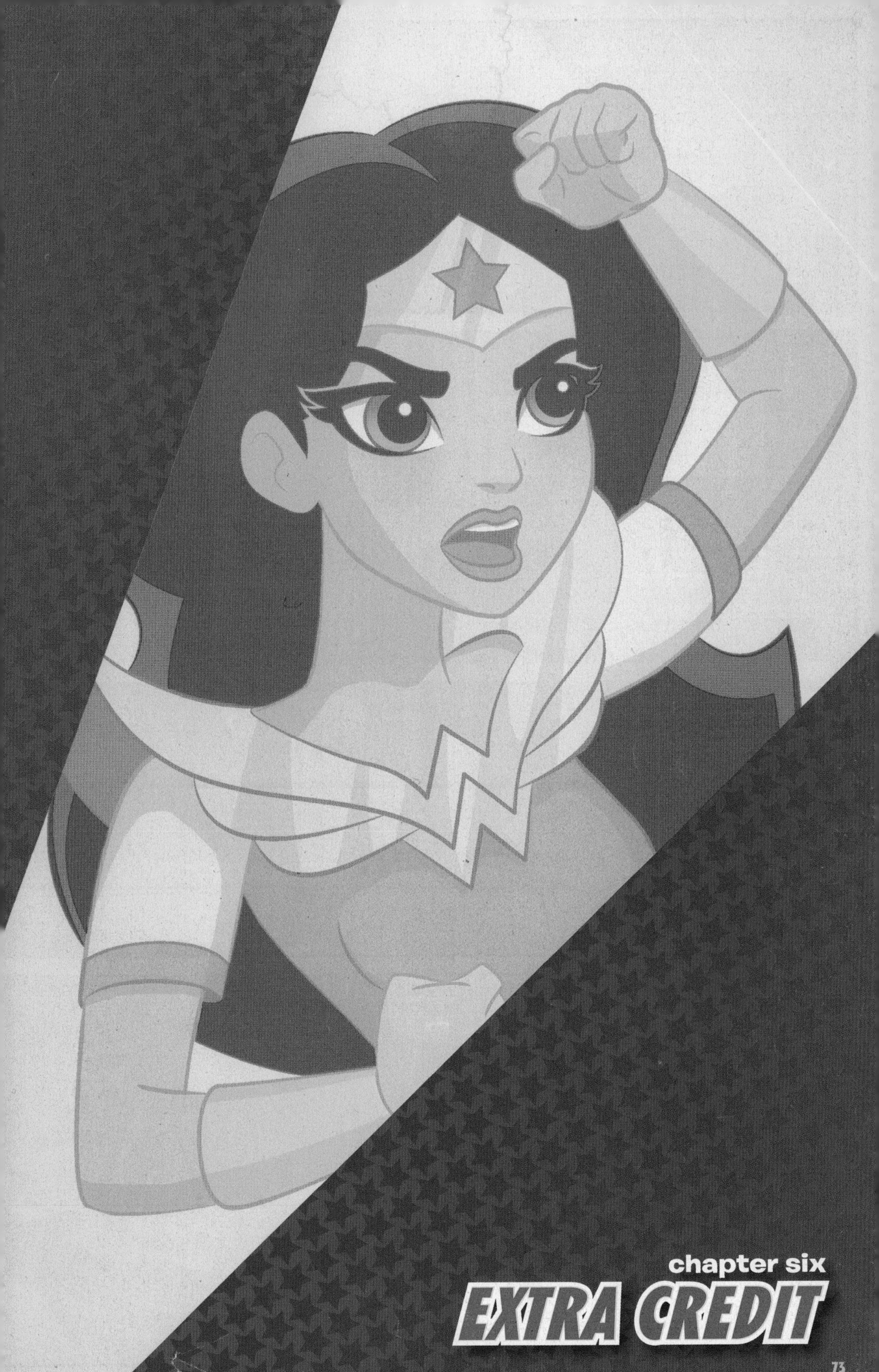

chapter six

EXTRA CREDIT

METROPOLIS IS SO DIFFERENT FROM THEMYSCIRA, THE ISLAND WHERE I GREW UP.

THE CITY'S FULL OF CONTRADICTIONS. THE DARKNESS OF THE NIGHT ALLOWS US TO SEE THE BEAUTY OF THE CITY LIGHTS--

--BUT IT ALSO HIDES THE DANGER THAT LURKS AT NIGHT.

WELL, DANGER *USUALLY* LURKS AT NIGHT. TONIGHT'S BEEN SLOW.

HOW DID YOU DO ON MISTER FOX'S WEAPONOMICS POP QUIZ?

100 PERCENT.

I ELEVATED THE COMMON CORE QUIZ TO EXTRAORDINAR HEIGHTS WITH MY PERFECT ANSWERS!

GUESS THAT MEANS WE'RE STILL TIED FOR TOP OF THE CLASS.

AT LEAST UNTIL FINALS TOMORROW.

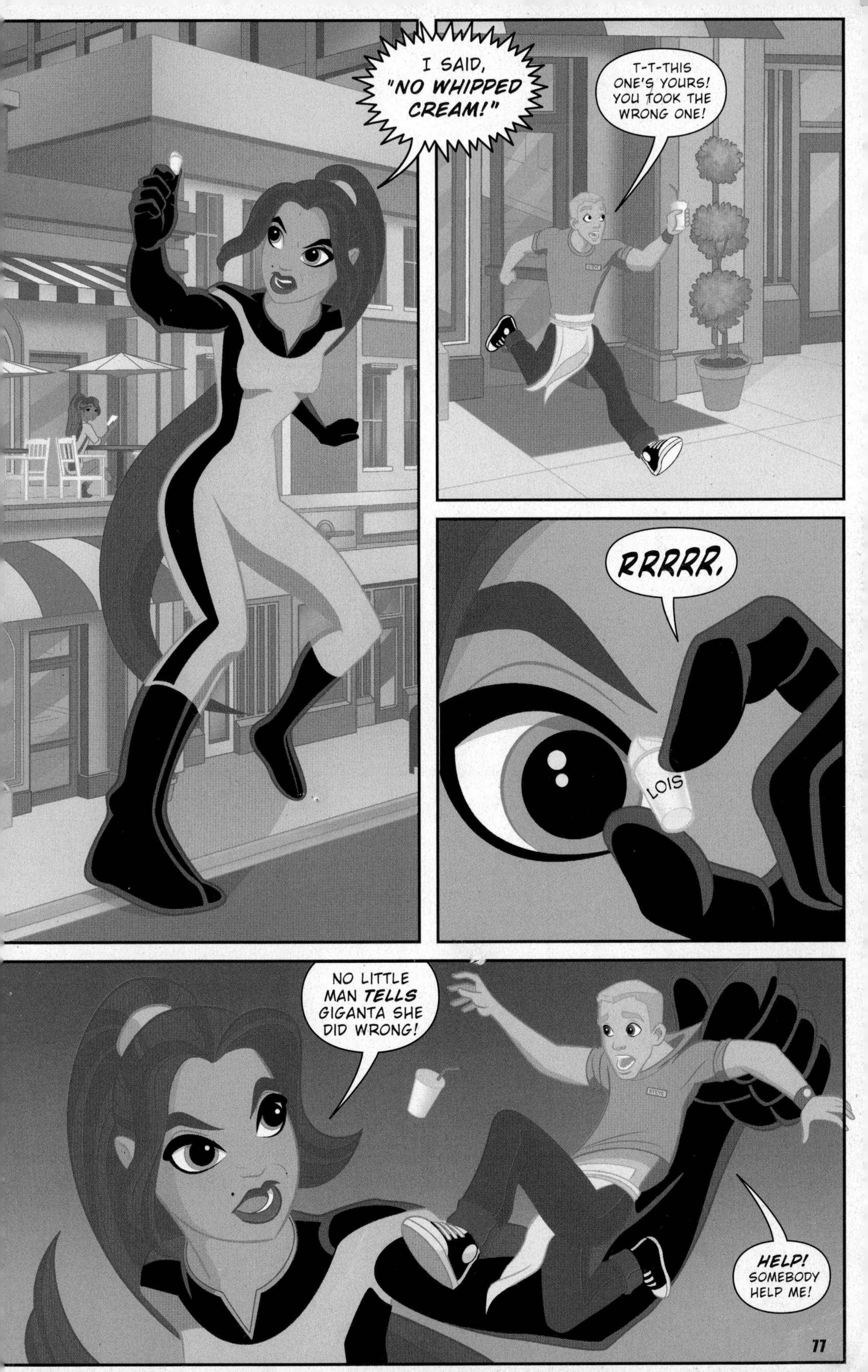
I SAID, "NO WHIPPED CREAM!"
T-T-THIS ONE'S YOURS! YOU TOOK THE WRONG ONE!
RRRRR.
LOIS
NO LITTLE MAN TELLS GIGANTA SHE DID WRONG!
HELP! SOMEBODY HELP ME!

HUH?!

PUT STEVE TREVOR DOWN!

OKAY.

AYYYY!!!!!!

I'M ALWAYS FALLING FOR YOU. I MEAN, YOU'RE ALWAYS CATCHING ME!

LIKE, I MEAN, YOU'RE A GOOD SUPER HERO AND I LIKE HOW BRAVE AND HOW STRONG YOU ARE...

I MEAN, *THANK YOU*.

YOU'RE WELCOME!

WOW! GO, WONDER WOMAN!

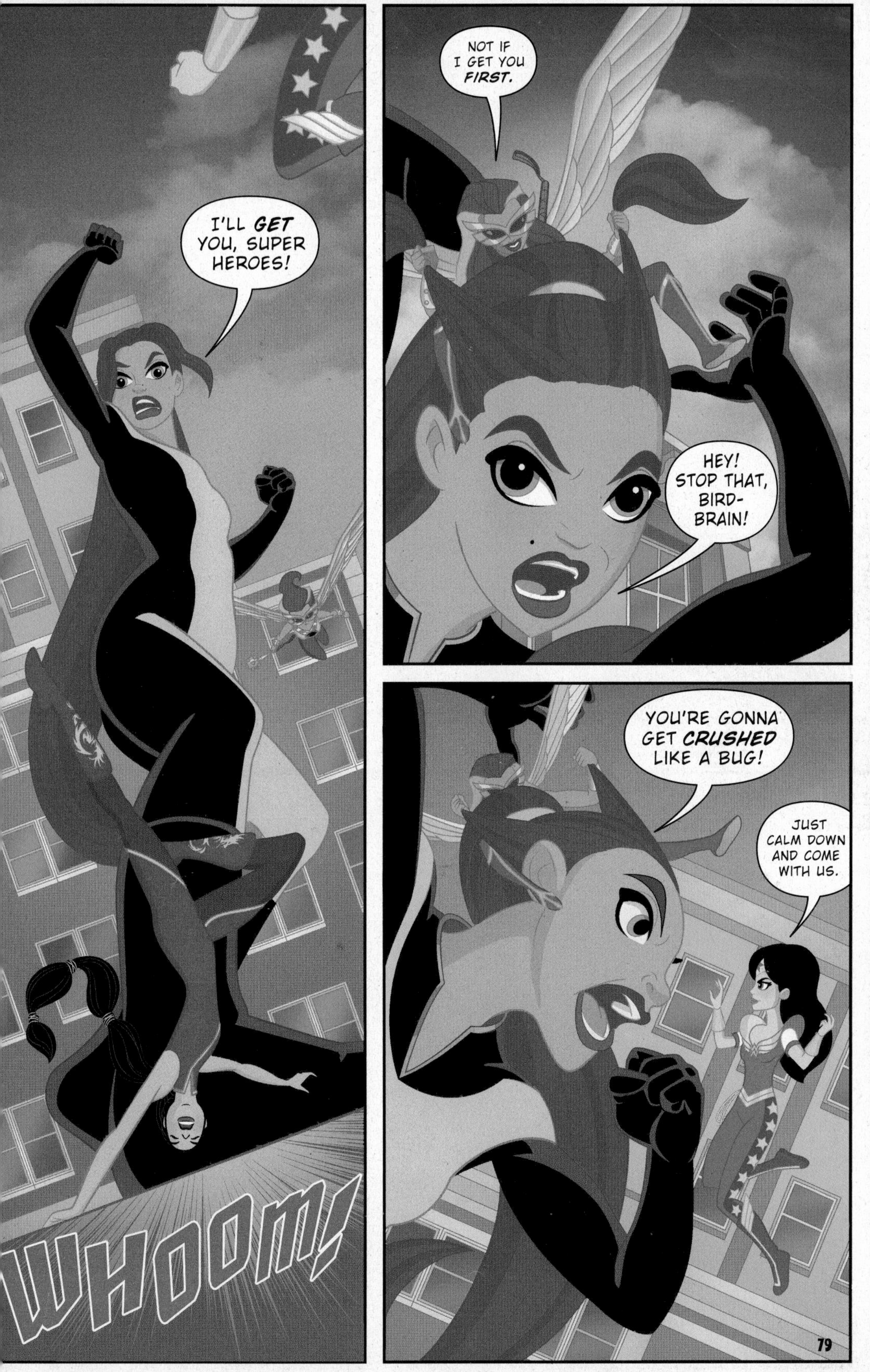
I'LL GET YOU, SUPER HEROES!
WHOOM!
NOT IF I GET YOU FIRST.
HEY! STOP THAT, BIRD-BRAIN!
YOU'RE GONNA GET CRUSHED LIKE A BUG!
JUST CALM DOWN AND COME WITH US.

WONDER WOMAN HAS BROUGHT OUT THE LASSO OF TRUTH!

FANS WILL RECALL THAT WONDER WOMAN HOLDS THE ALL-TIME LASSOING RECORD.

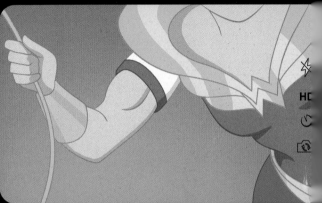

SHE AIMS FOR GIGANTA...

...AND SHE THROWS!

SWOOOSH

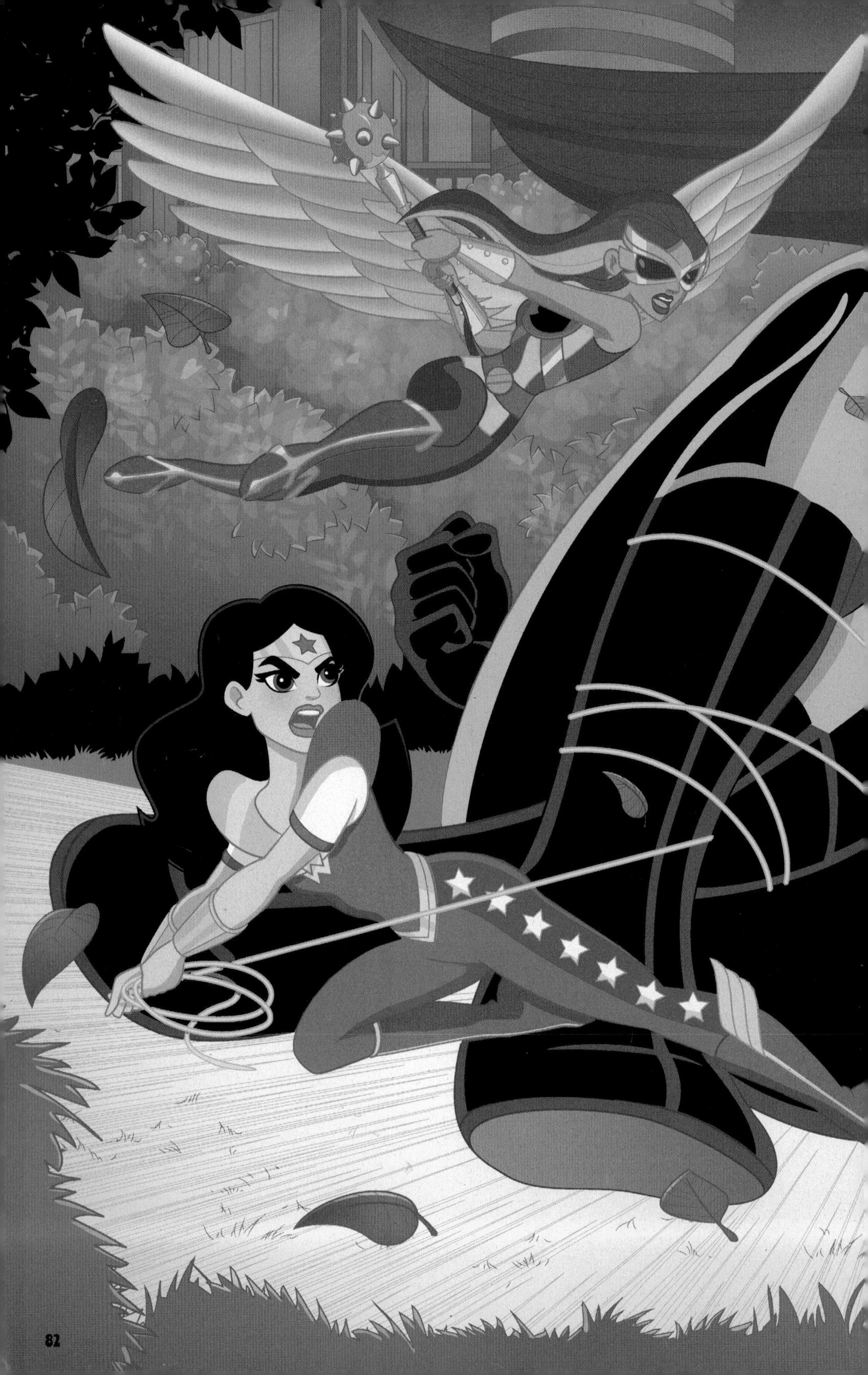

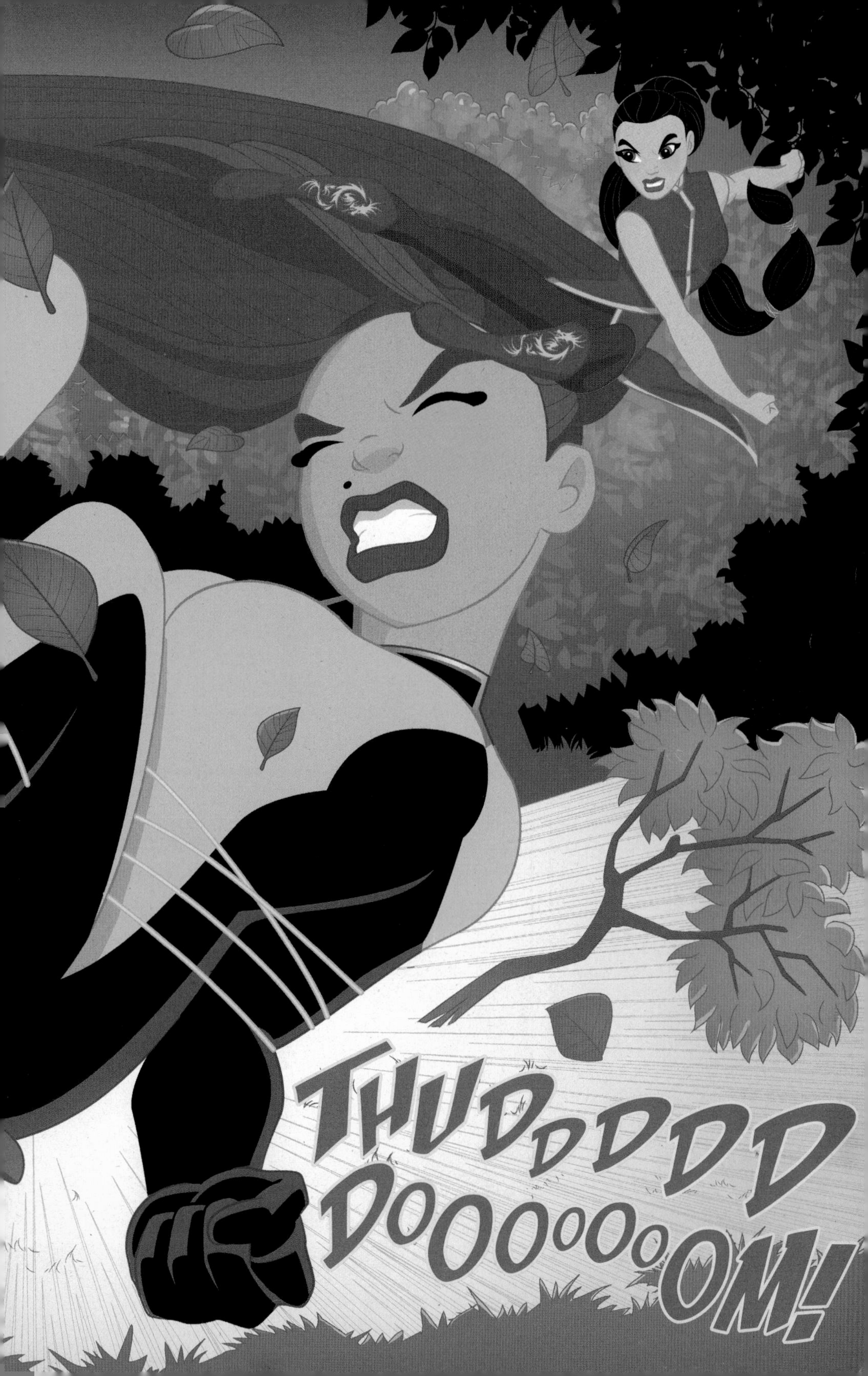
THUDDDDD
DOOOOOOOM!

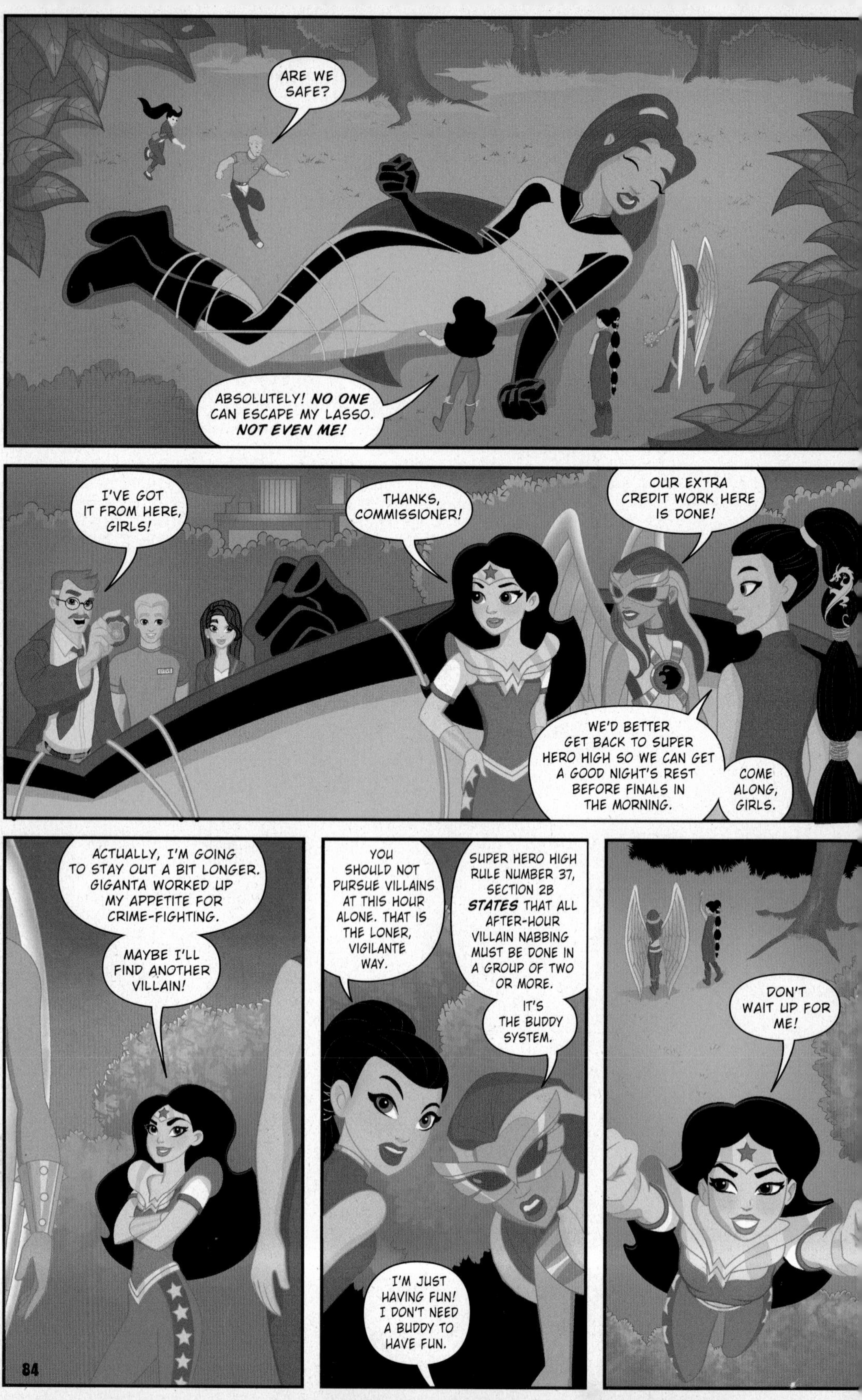
ARE WE SAFE?
ABSOLUTELY! NO ONE CAN ESCAPE MY LASSO. NOT EVEN ME!
I'VE GOT IT FROM HERE, GIRLS!
THANKS, COMMISSIONER!
OUR EXTRA CREDIT WORK HERE IS DONE!
WE'D BETTER GET BACK TO SUPER HERO HIGH SO WE CAN GET A GOOD NIGHT'S REST BEFORE FINALS IN THE MORNING.
COME ALONG, GIRLS.
ACTUALLY, I'M GOING TO STAY OUT A BIT LONGER. GIGANTA WORKED UP MY APPETITE FOR CRIME-FIGHTING.
MAYBE I'LL FIND ANOTHER VILLAIN!
YOU SHOULD NOT PURSUE VILLAINS AT THIS HOUR ALONE. THAT IS THE LONER, VIGILANTE WAY.
SUPER HERO HIGH RULE NUMBER 37, SECTION 2B STATES THAT ALL AFTER-HOUR VILLAIN NABBING MUST BE DONE IN A GROUP OF TWO OR MORE.
IT'S THE BUDDY SYSTEM.
I'M JUST HAVING FUN! I DON'T NEED A BUDDY TO HAVE FUN.
DON'T WAIT UP FOR ME!

THIS IS METROPOLIS. THERE HAS TO BE SOME CRIME TO STOP.

BANK ROBBERY? TRAFFIC VIOLATION? *ANYTHING?*

YOU HEAR ABOUT ANY *CRIME*, PUPSTER?

HELP! SOMEBODY HELP ME!

STEVE? I'M COMING FOR YOU!

HELP! SOMEBODY HELP ME!

HELP! SOMEBODY HELP ME!

STEVE! WHERE ARE YOU?

HELP! SOMEBODY HELP ME!

85

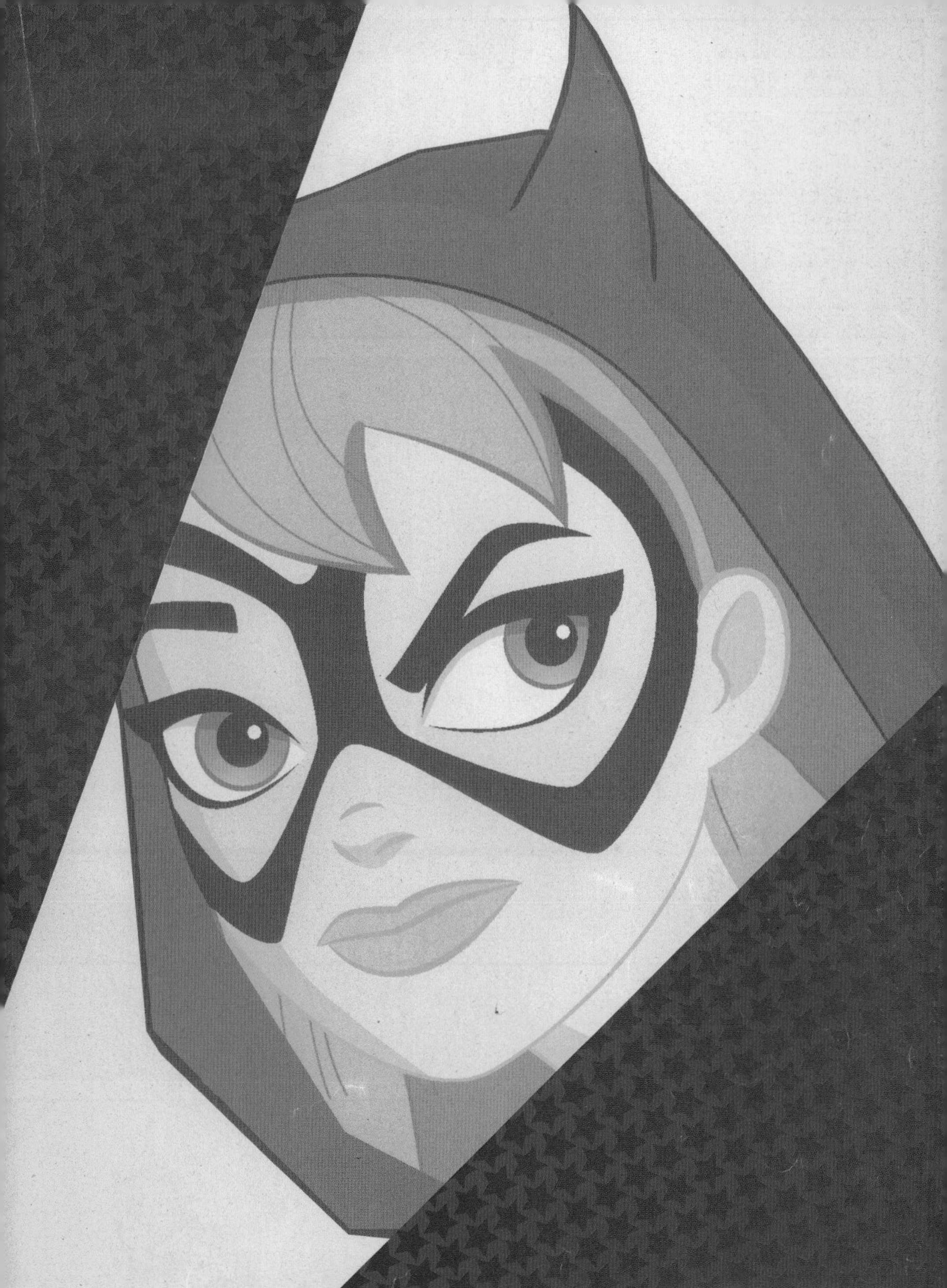

chapter seven

KEEPING THE PEACE AND QUIET

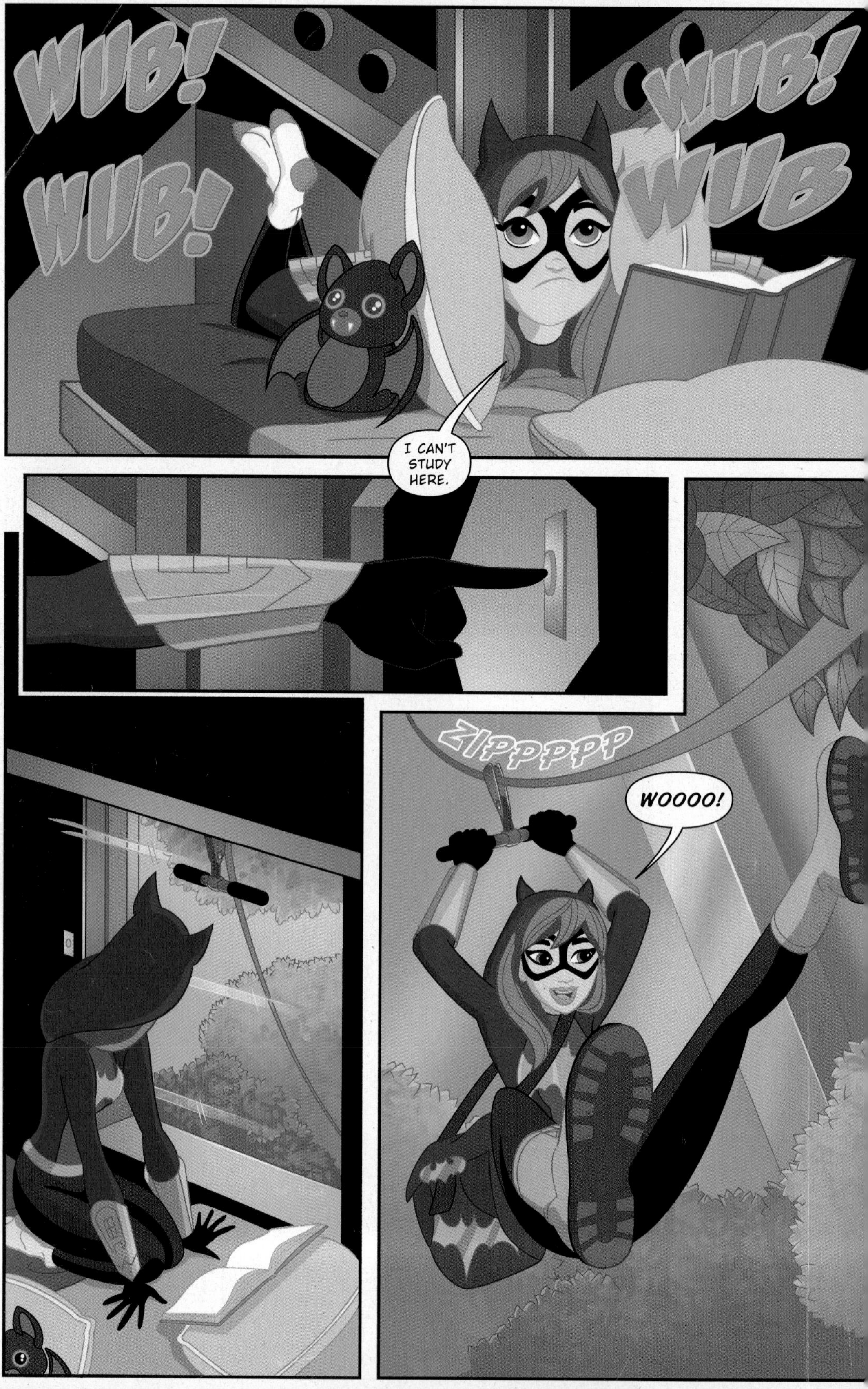
WUB!
WUB!
WUB!
WUB
I CAN'T STUDY HERE.
ZIPPPPP
WOOOO!

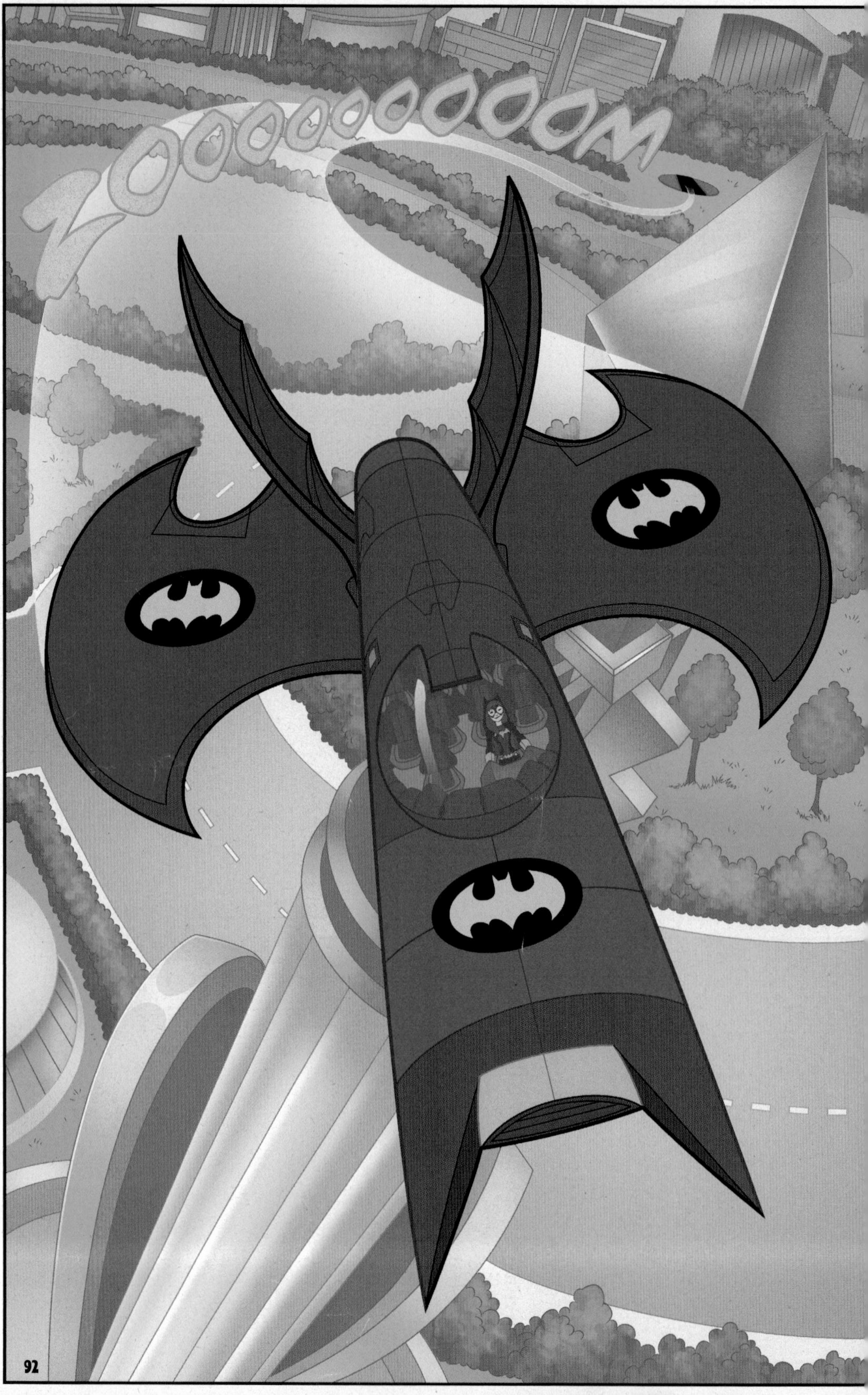
ZOOOOOOOOOM

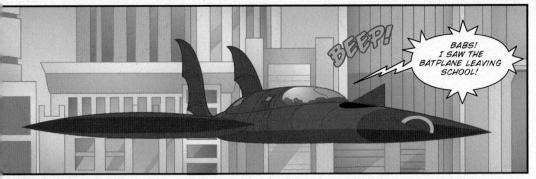

BEEP!

BABS! I SAW THE BATPLANE LEAVING SCHOOL!

WHY AREN'T YOU STUDYING?

I'M *TRYING* TO, DAD!

IT WAS *TOO LOUD* THERE!

"BUT DON'T WORRY. I'M HEADED TO THE PERFECT STUDY SPOT!"

WELCOME, BATGIRL.

TO--

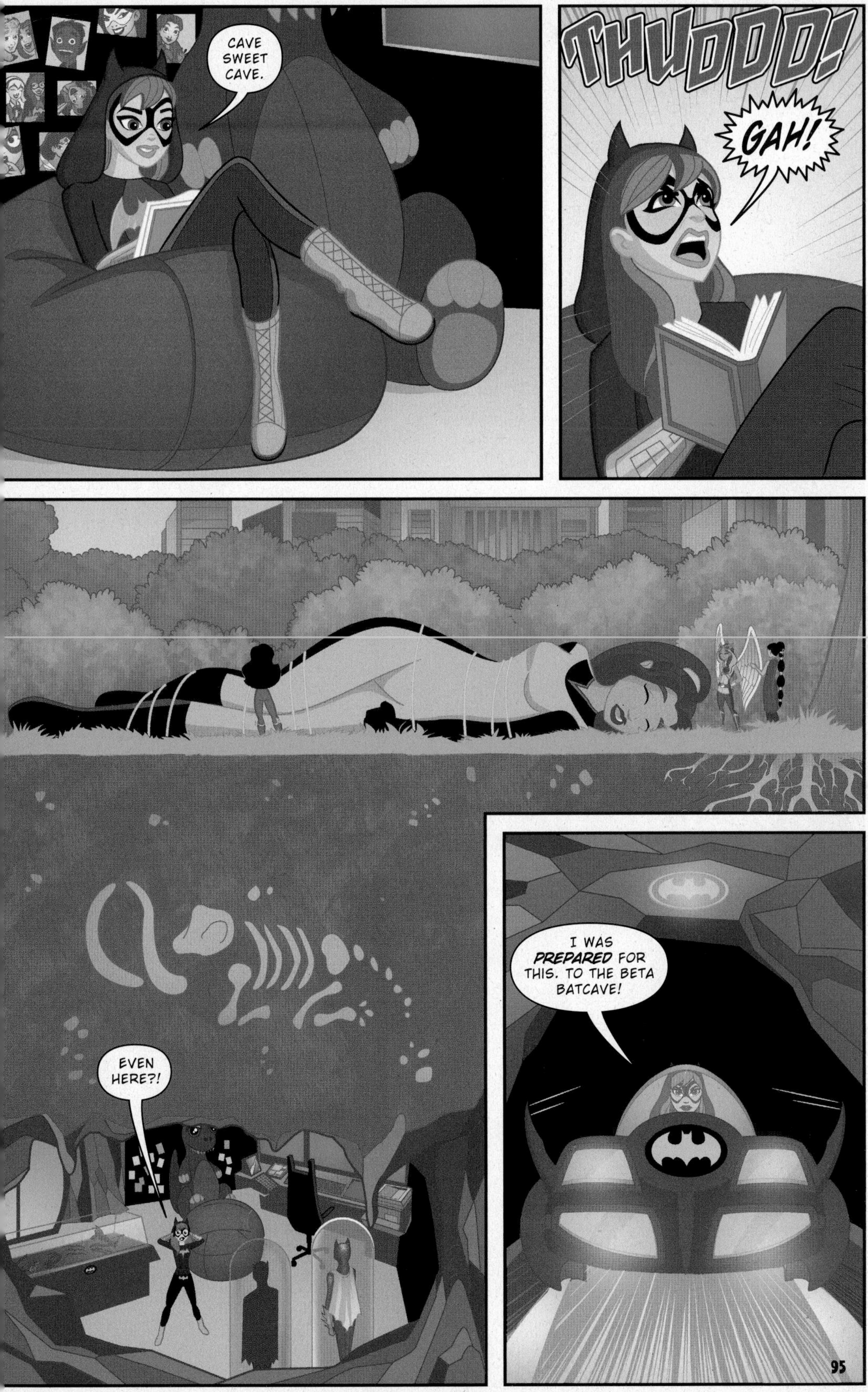

CAVE SWEET CAVE.
THUDDD!
GAH!
EVEN HERE?!
I WAS PREPARED FOR THIS. TO THE BETA BATCAVE!

MY BACKUP TO MY BATCAVE. I HAVE A FEW AROUND TOWN.

FINALLY, I CAN STUDY.

CLANK! CLANK! CLANK!

WHAT'S GOING ON UP THERE?

KLANG!

ELEPHANTS PLAYING FOOTBALL?

LEXCOR GARDEN SUPPL

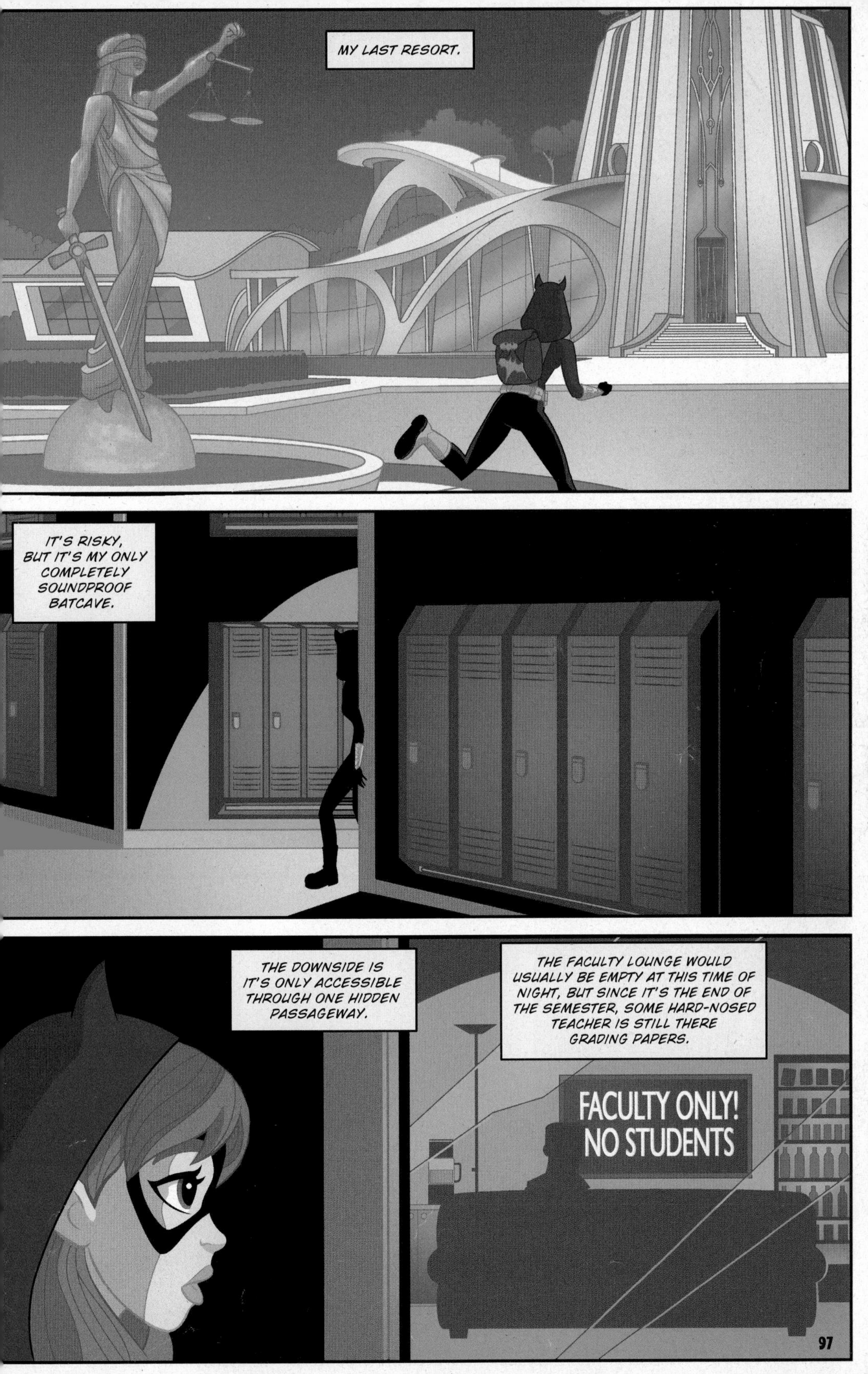
MY LAST RESORT.
IT'S RISKY, BUT IT'S MY ONLY COMPLETELY SOUNDPROOF BATCAVE.
THE DOWNSIDE IS IT'S ONLY ACCESSIBLE THROUGH ONE HIDDEN PASSAGEWAY.
THE FACULTY LOUNGE WOULD USUALLY BE EMPTY AT THIS TIME OF NIGHT, BUT SINCE IT'S THE END OF THE SEMESTER, SOME HARD-NOSED TEACHER IS STILL THERE GRADING PAPERS.
FACULTY ONLY! NO STUDENTS

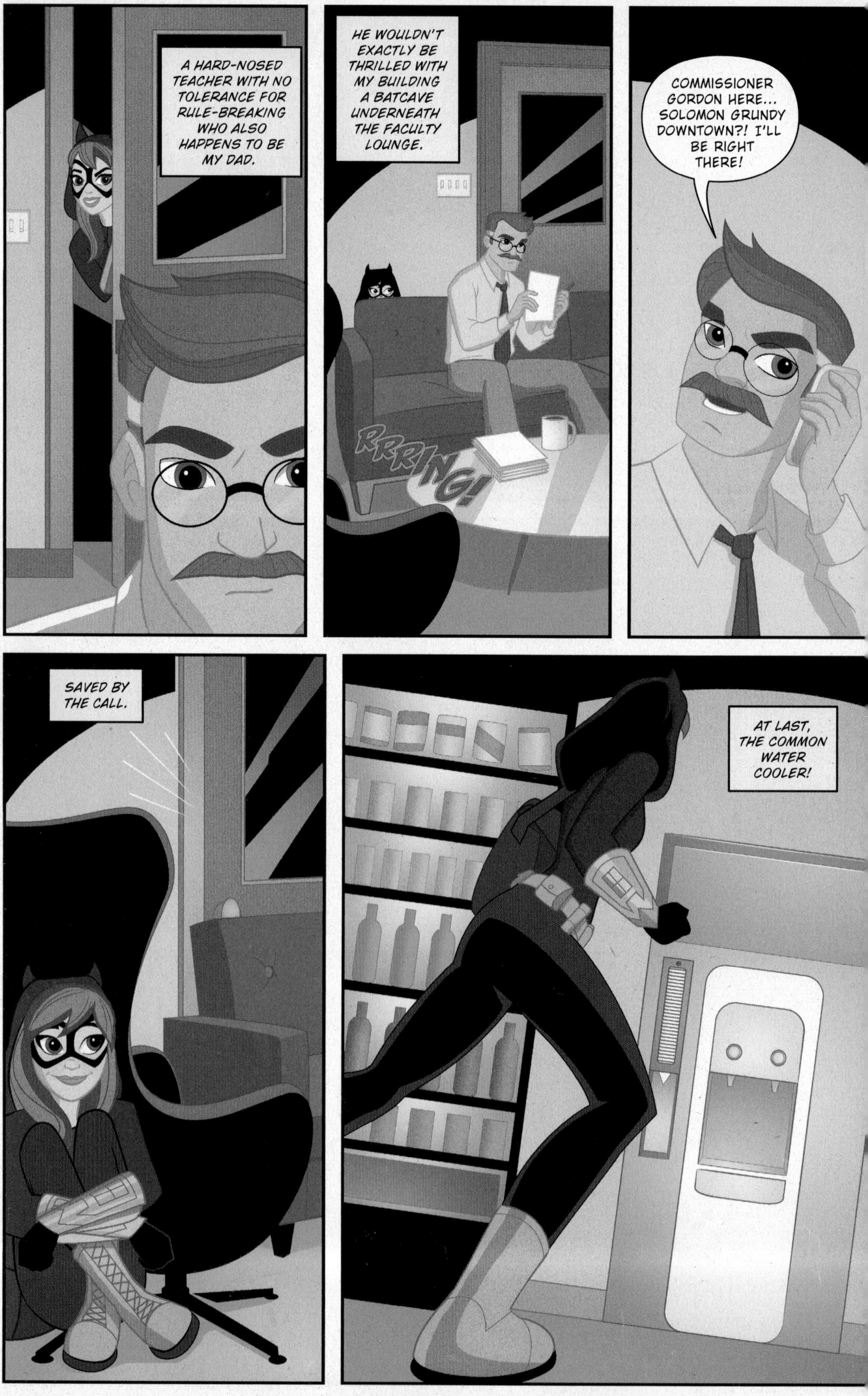
A HARD-NOSED TEACHER WITH NO TOLERANCE FOR RULE-BREAKING WHO ALSO HAPPENS TO BE MY DAD.
HE WOULDN'T EXACTLY BE THRILLED WITH MY BUILDING A BATCAVE UNDERNEATH THE FACULTY LOUNGE.
RRRING!
COMMISSIONER GORDON HERE... SOLOMON GRUNDY DOWNTOWN?! I'LL BE RIGHT THERE!
SAVED BY THE CALL.
AT LAST, THE COMMON WATER COOLER!

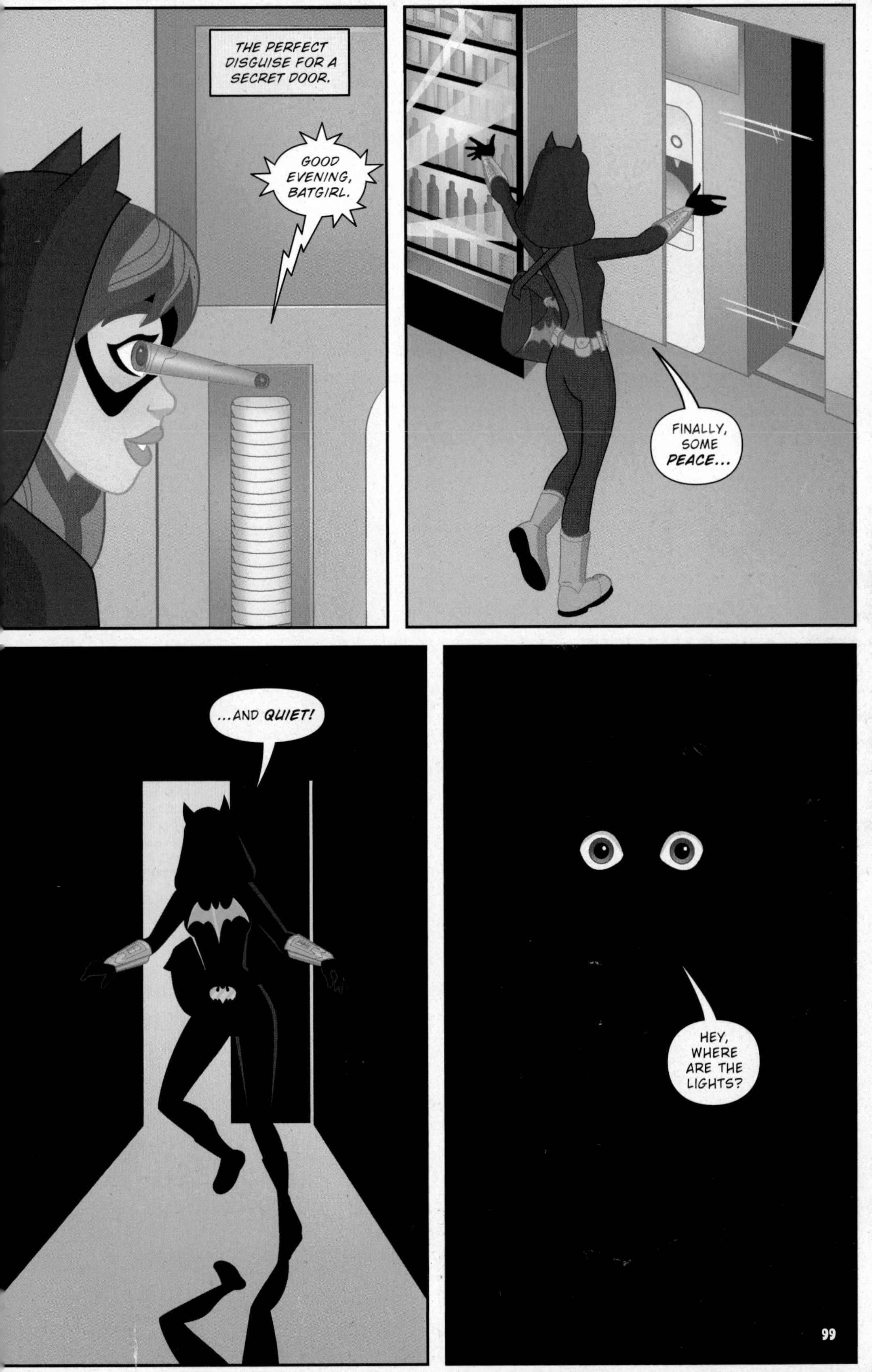
THE PERFECT DISGUISE FOR A SECRET DOOR.
GOOD EVENING, BATGIRL.
FINALLY, SOME PEACE...
...AND QUIET!
HEY, WHERE ARE THE LIGHTS?

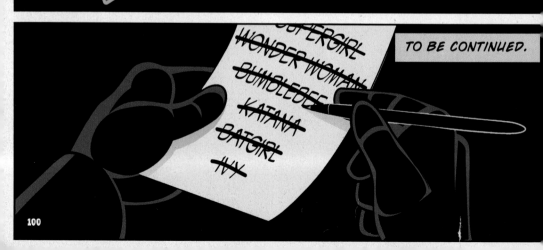

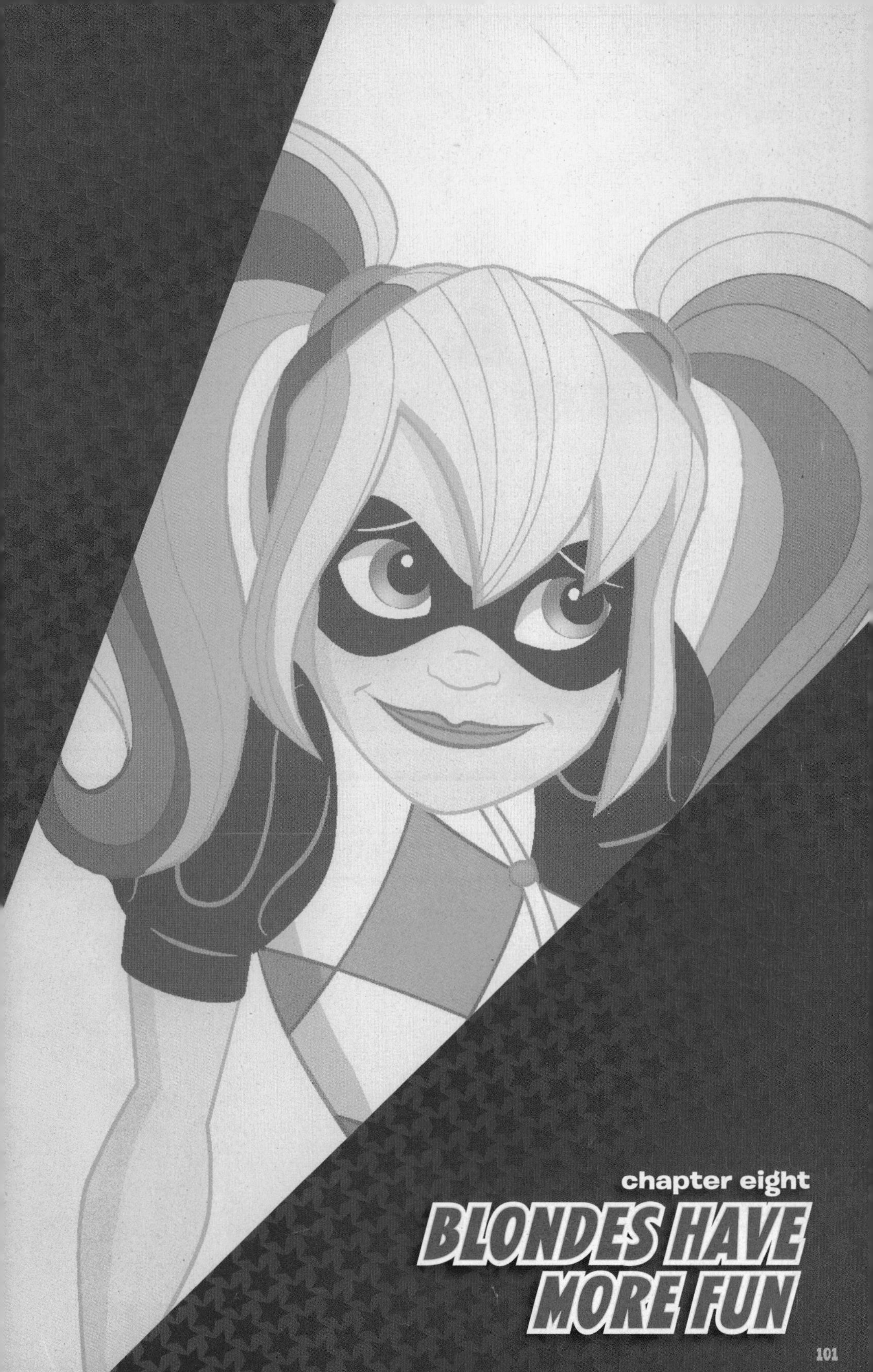

chapter eight

BLONDES HAVE MORE FUN

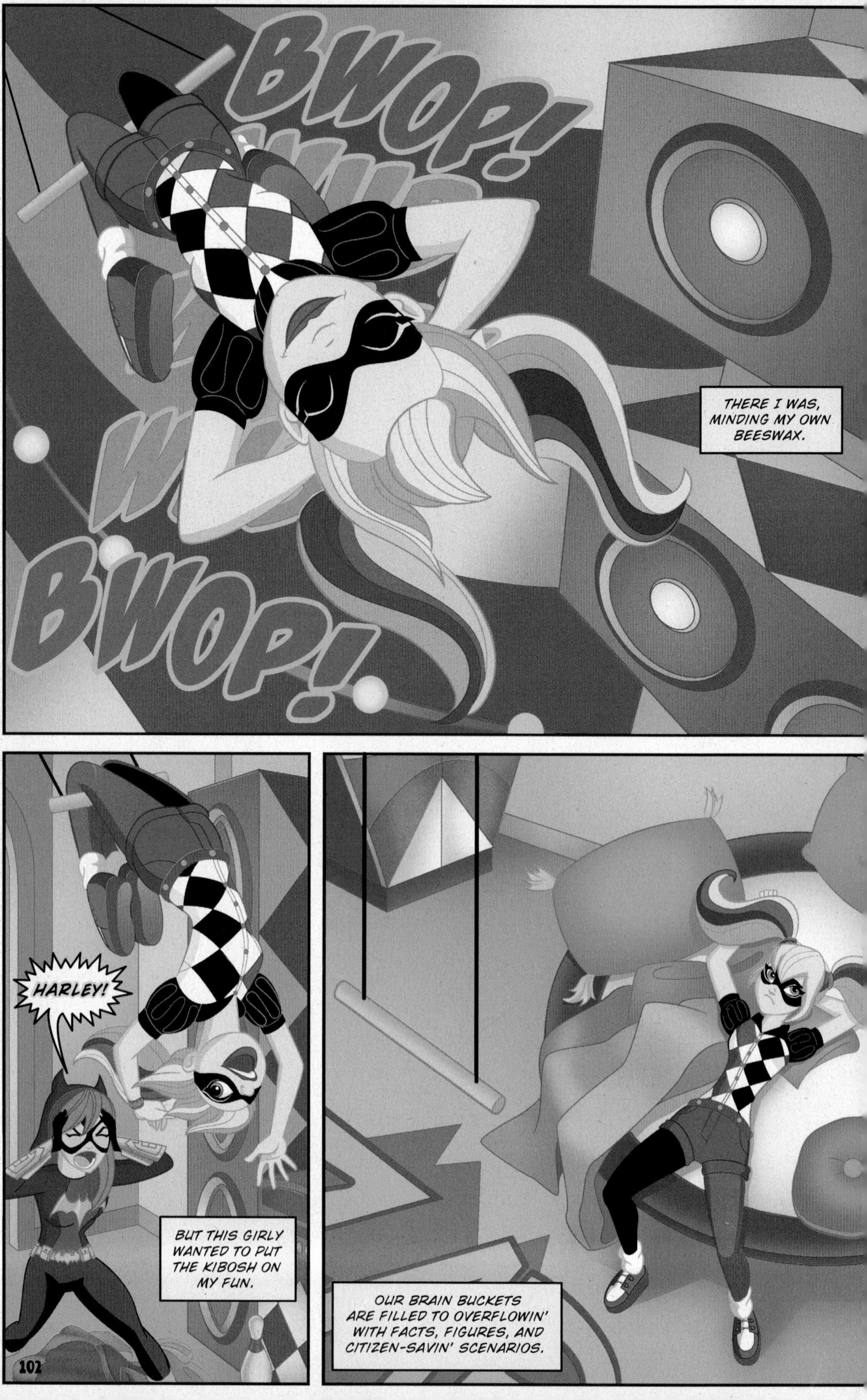
BWOP!
THERE I WAS, MINDING MY OWN BEESWAX.
BWOP!
HARLEY!
BUT THIS GIRLY WANTED TO PUT THE KIBOSH ON MY FUN.
OUR BRAIN BUCKETS ARE FILLED TO OVERFLOWIN' WITH FACTS, FIGURES, AND CITIZEN-SAVIN' SCENARIOS.

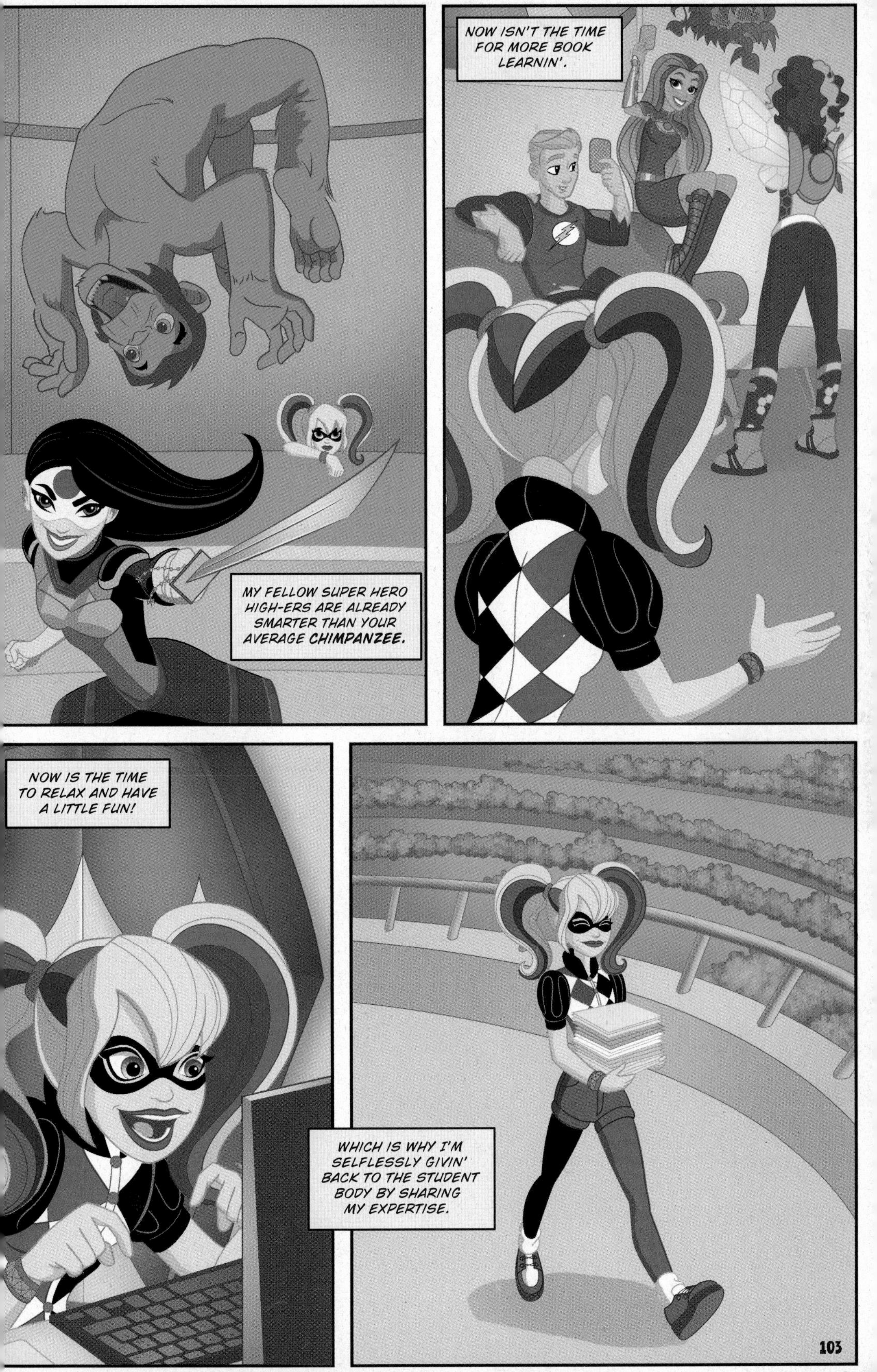
MY FELLOW SUPER HERO HIGH-ERS ARE ALREADY SMARTER THAN YOUR AVERAGE CHIMPANZEE.
NOW ISN'T THE TIME FOR MORE BOOK LEARNIN'.
NOW IS THE TIME TO RELAX AND HAVE A LITTLE FUN!
WHICH IS WHY I'M SELFLESSLY GIVIN' BACK TO THE STUDENT BODY BY SHARING MY EXPERTISE.

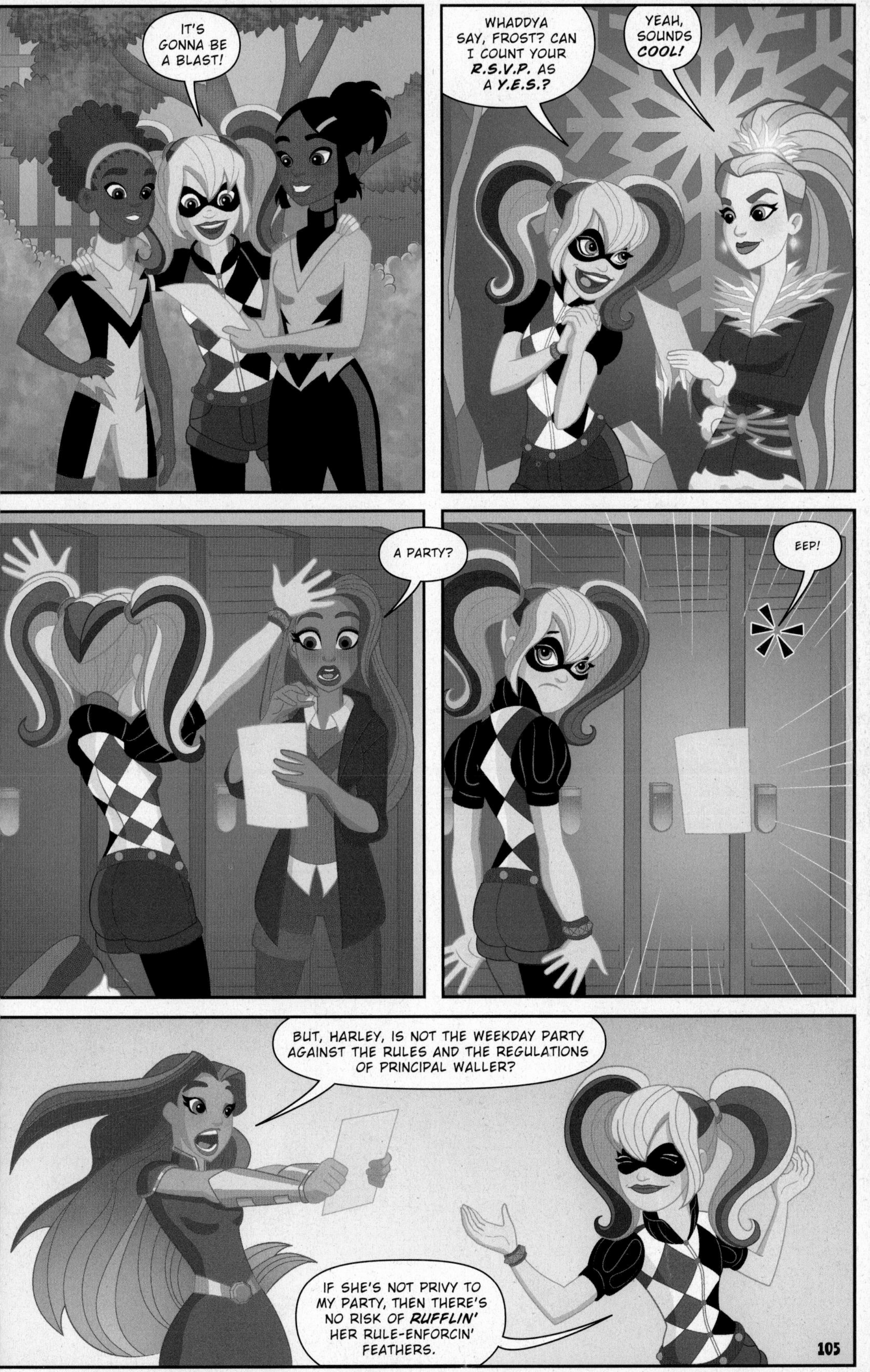

IT'S GONNA BE A BLAST!
WHADDYA SAY, FROST? CAN I COUNT YOUR **R.S.V.P.** AS A **Y.E.S.?**
YEAH, SOUNDS **COOL!**
A PARTY?
EEP!
BUT, HARLEY, IS NOT THE WEEKDAY PARTY AGAINST THE RULES AND THE REGULATIONS OF PRINCIPAL WALLER?
IF SHE'S NOT PRIVY TO MY PARTY, THEN THERE'S NO RISK OF **RUFFLIN'** HER RULE-ENFORCIN' FEATHERS.

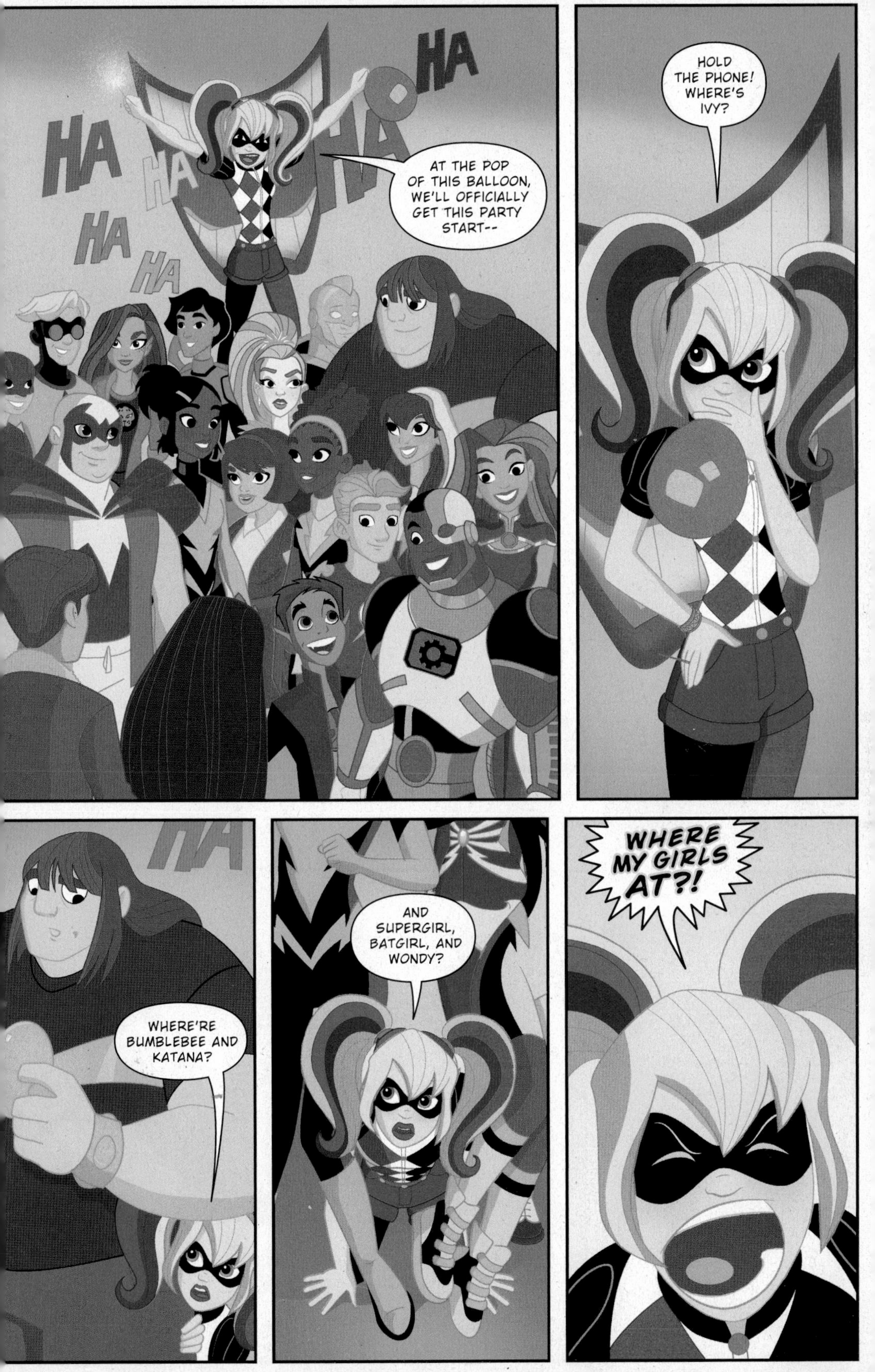
HA HA HA HA HA HA HA
AT THE POP OF THIS BALLOON, WE'LL OFFICIALLY GET THIS PARTY START--
HOLD THE PHONE! WHERE'S IVY?
WHERE'RE BUMBLEBEE AND KATANA?
AND SUPERGIRL, BATGIRL, AND WONDY?
WHERE MY GIRLS AT?!

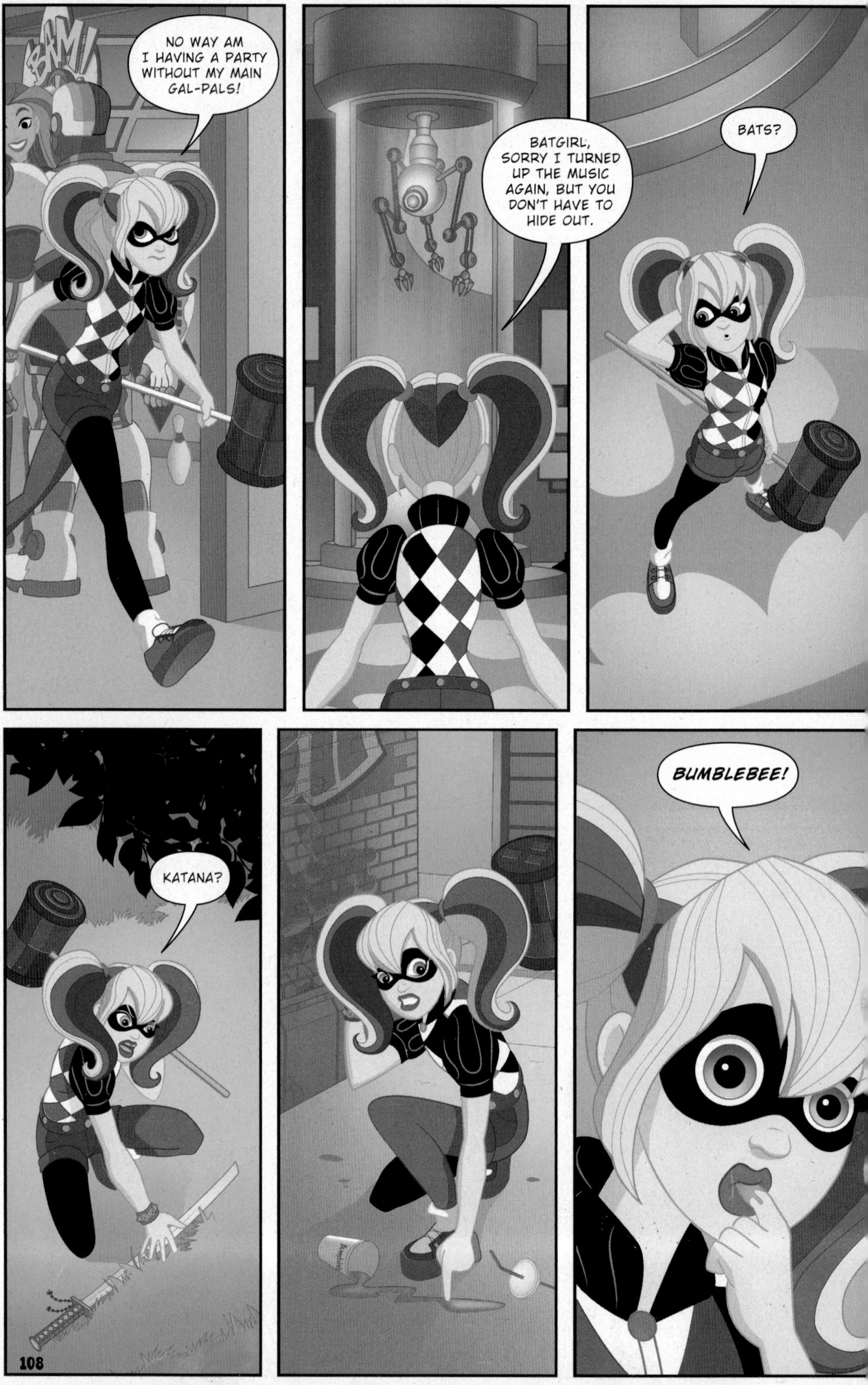
BAM!
NO WAY AM I HAVING A PARTY WITHOUT MY MAIN GAL-PALS!
BATGIRL, SORRY I TURNED UP THE MUSIC AGAIN, BUT YOU DON'T HAVE TO HIDE OUT.
BATS?
KATANA?
BUMBLEBEE!

THERE'S SOMETHING FUNNY HAPPENING IN METROPOLIS AND NOBODY DOES **FUNNY** WITHOUT HARLEY QUINN!

RINNG!

RINNG!

SHUT OFF THAT ALARM! I'M TRYING TO THINK.

RINNG! RINNG!

SOLOMON GRUNDY?

HOLD IT RIGHT THERE, SLOWPOKE!

$

$

TRYIN' TO GET AWAY FROM ME?

YOU'RE GONNA GET POPPED, PUDDIN'!

-UGH!

POWF!

$

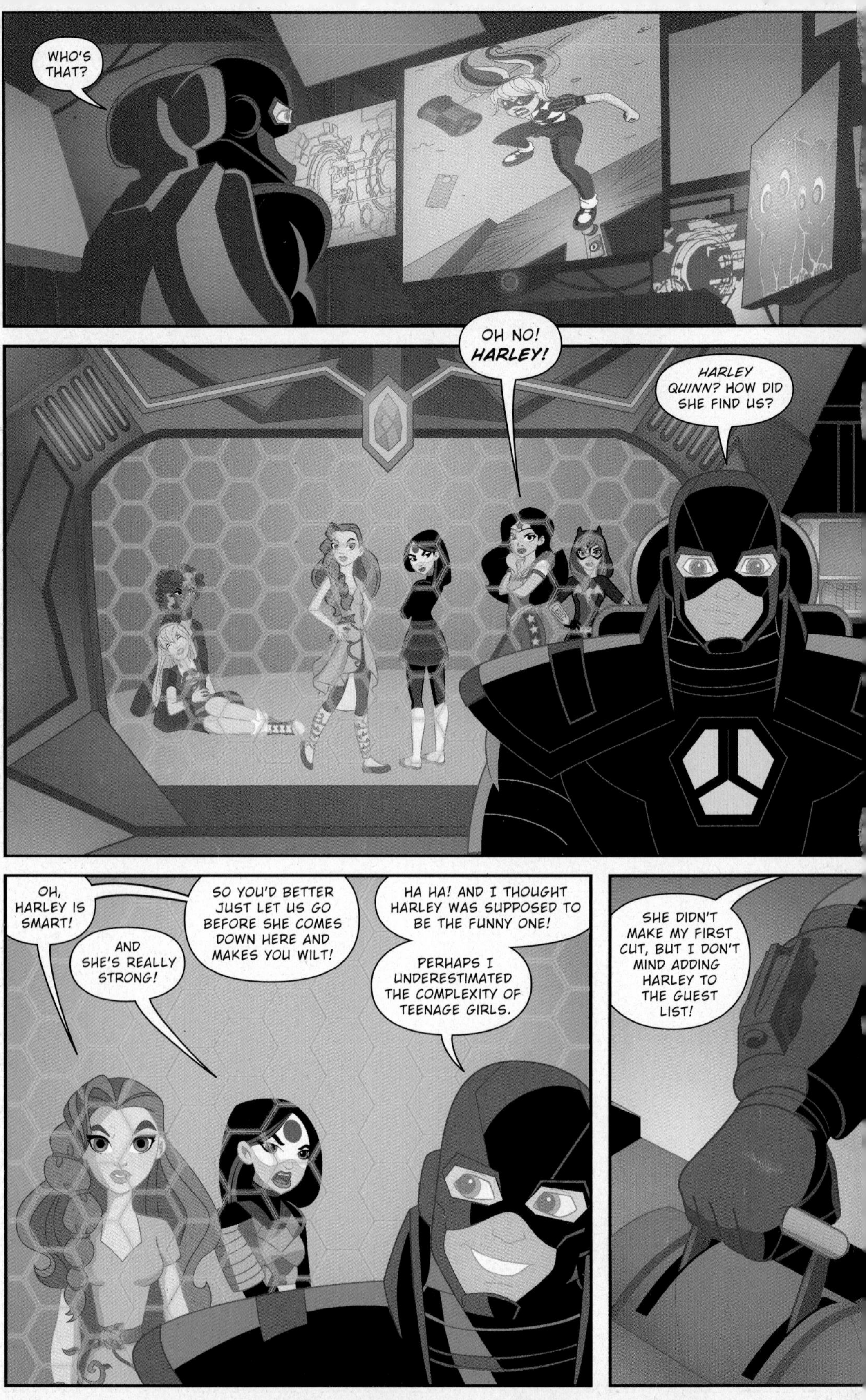
WHO'S THAT?
OH NO! HARLEY!
HARLEY QUINN? HOW DID SHE FIND US?
OH, HARLEY IS SMART!
AND SHE'S REALLY STRONG!
SO YOU'D BETTER JUST LET US GO BEFORE SHE COMES DOWN HERE AND MAKES YOU WILT!
HA HA! AND I THOUGHT HARLEY WAS SUPPOSED TO BE THE FUNNY ONE!
PERHAPS I UNDERESTIMATED THE COMPLEXITY OF TEENAGE GIRLS.
SHE DIDN'T MAKE MY FIRST CUT, BUT I DON'T MIND ADDING HARLEY TO THE GUEST LIST!

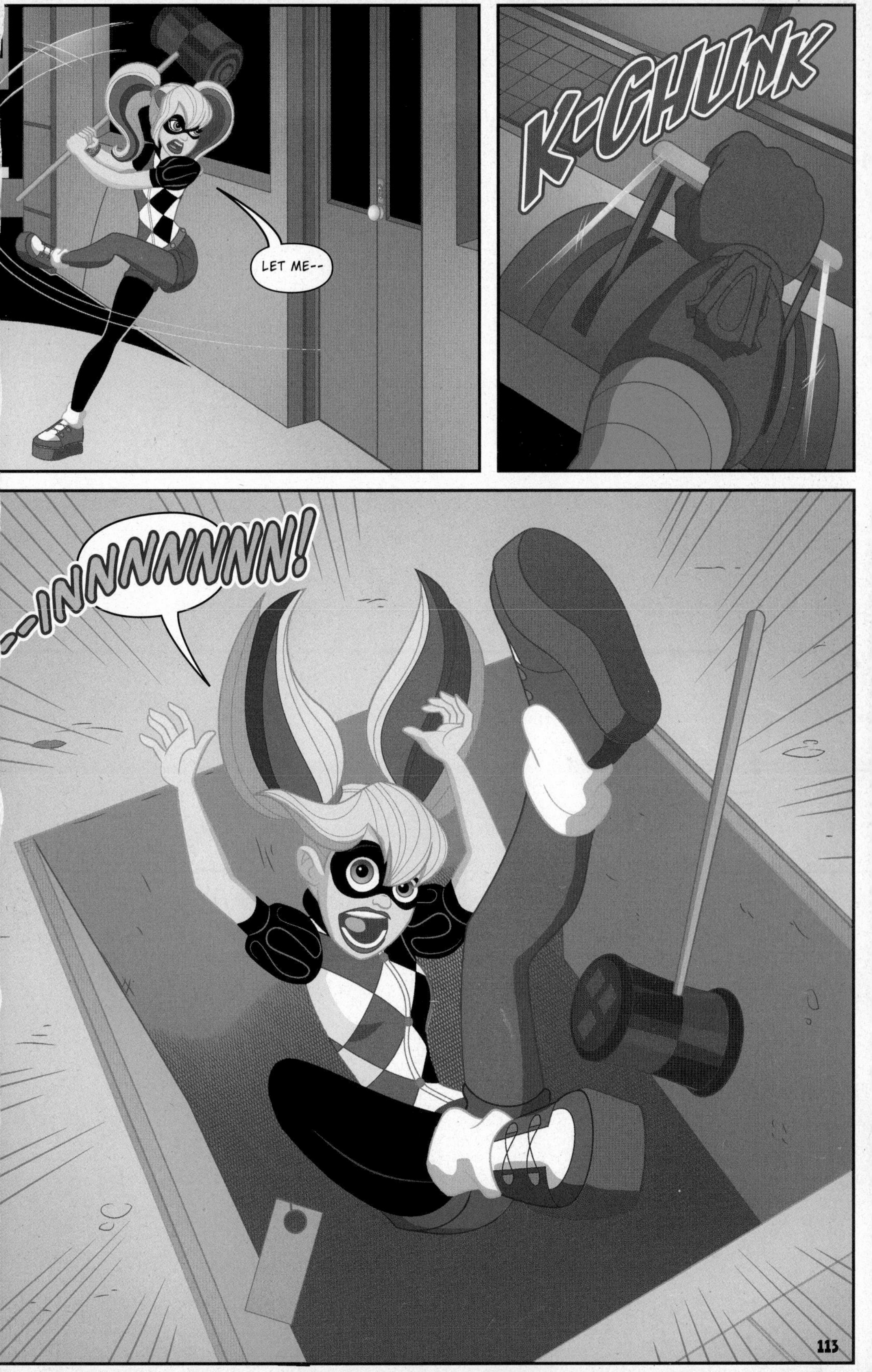
LET ME--
K-CHUNK
--INNNNNNNN!

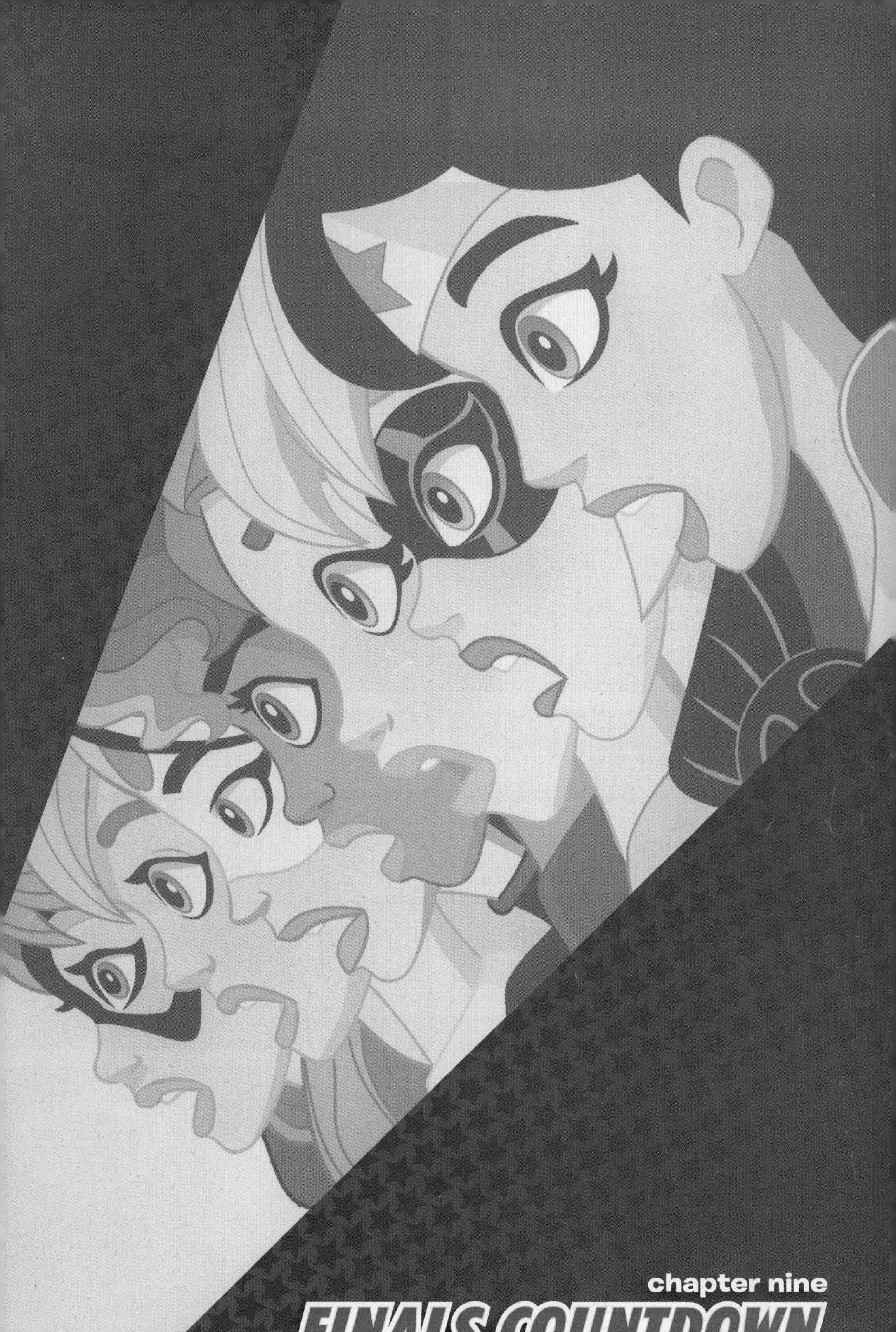

chapter nine

FINALS COUNTDOWN

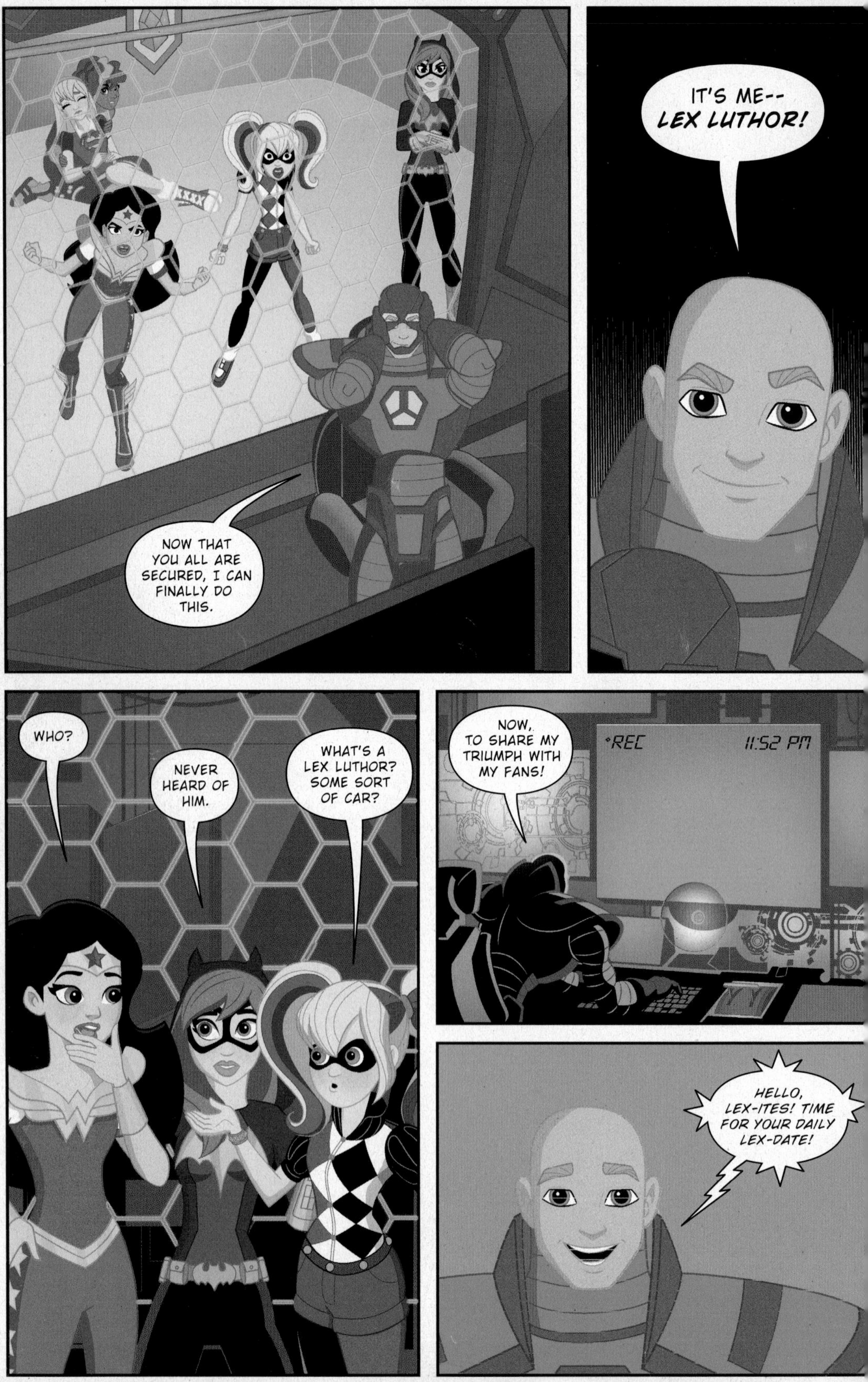
NOW THAT YOU ALL ARE SECURED, I CAN FINALLY DO THIS.
IT'S ME-- LEX LUTHOR!
WHO?
NEVER HEARD OF HIM.
WHAT'S A LEX LUTHOR? SOME SORT OF CAR?
NOW, TO SHARE MY TRIUMPH WITH MY FANS!
•REC
11:52 PM
HELLO, LEX-ITES! TIME FOR YOUR DAILY LEX-DATE!

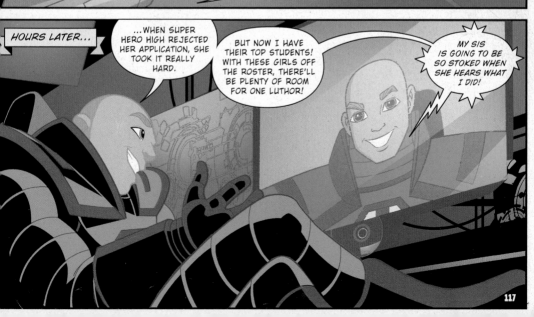

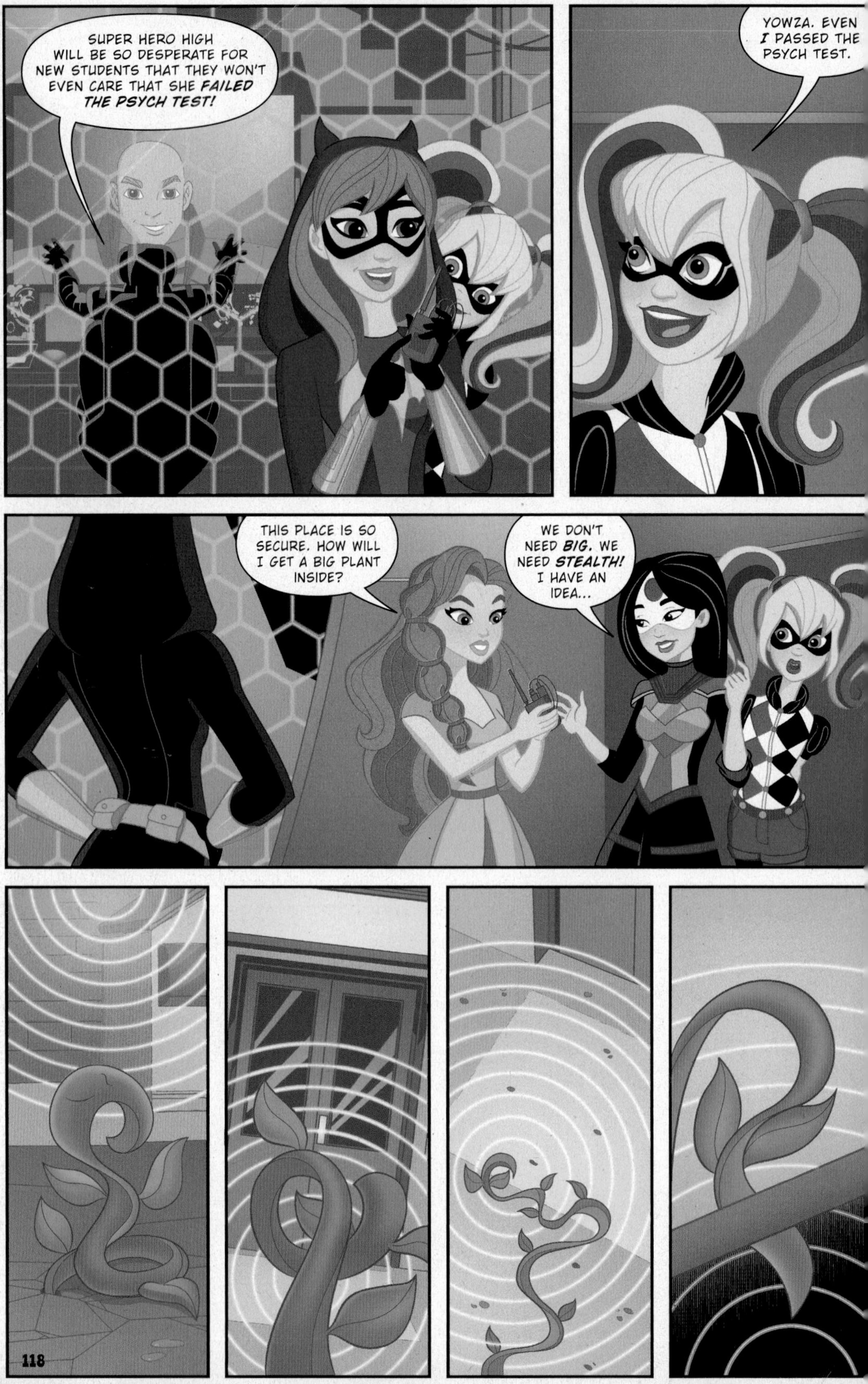
SUPER HERO HIGH WILL BE SO DESPERATE FOR NEW STUDENTS THAT THEY WON'T EVEN CARE THAT SHE ***FAILED THE PSYCH TEST!***
YOWZA. EVEN ***I*** PASSED THE PSYCH TEST.
THIS PLACE IS SO SECURE. HOW WILL I GET A BIG PLANT INSIDE?
WE DON'T NEED ***BIG.*** WE NEED ***STEALTH!*** I HAVE AN IDEA...

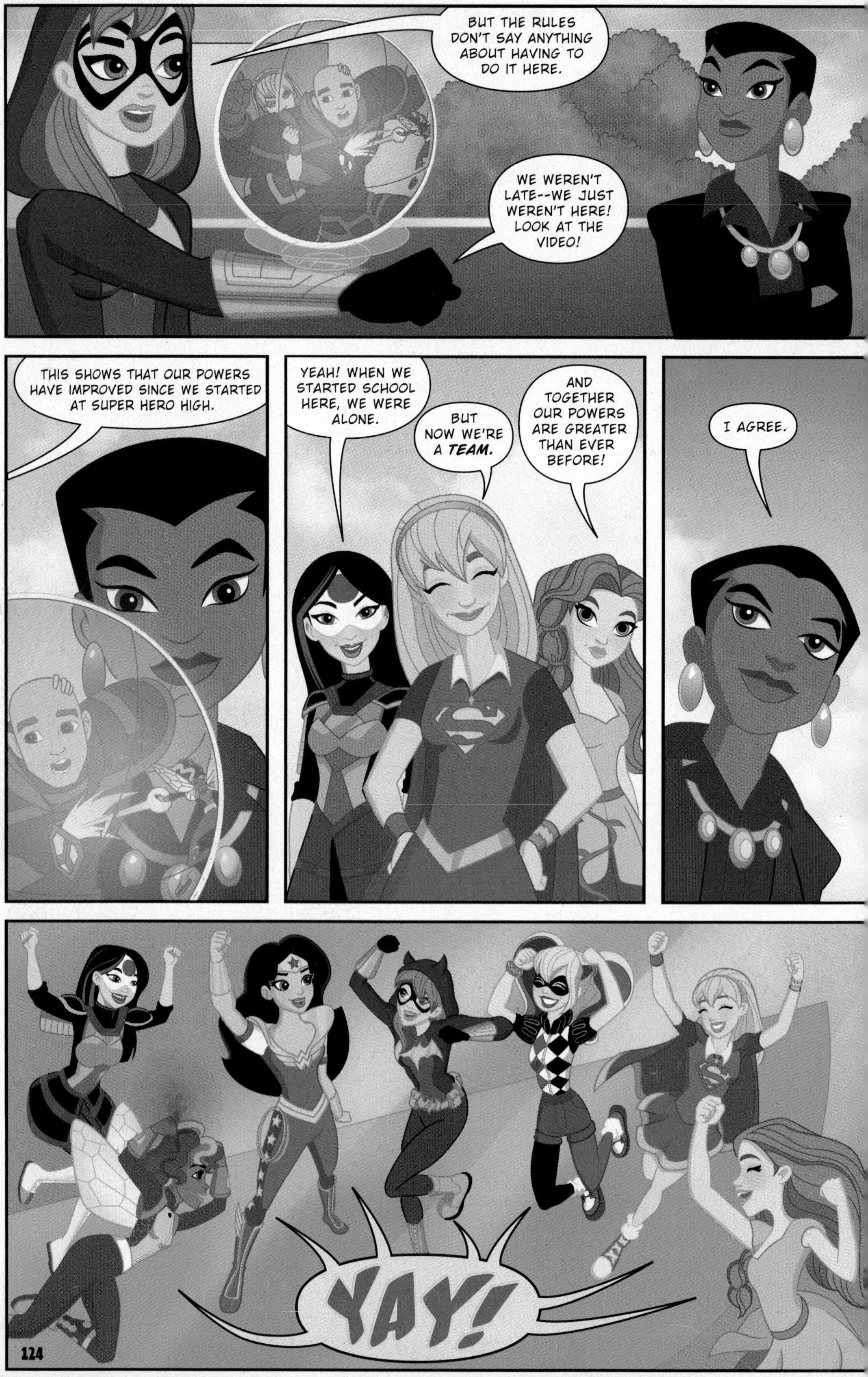
BUT THE RULES DON'T SAY ANYTHING ABOUT HAVING TO DO IT HERE.
WE WEREN'T LATE--WE JUST WEREN'T HERE! LOOK AT THE VIDEO!
THIS SHOWS THAT OUR POWERS HAVE IMPROVED SINCE WE STARTED AT SUPER HERO HIGH.
YEAH! WHEN WE STARTED SCHOOL HERE, WE WERE ALONE.
BUT NOW WE'RE A ***TEAM.***
AND TOGETHER OUR POWERS ARE GREATER THAN EVER BEFORE!
I AGREE.
YAY!

THE END.

about the
AUTHOR

Shea Fontana is a writer for film, television, and graphic novels. Her credits include *DC Super Hero Girls* animated shorts, television specials, and movies, *Dorothy and the Wonders of Oz*, *Doc McStuffins*, *The 7D*, *Whisker Haven Tales with the Palace Pets*, *Disney on Ice*, and the feature film *Crowning Jules*. She lives in sunny Los Angeles where she enjoys playing roller derby, hiking, hanging out with her dog, Moxie, and changing her hair color. ★

about the
COLORIST

Monica Kubina has colored countless comics, including super hero series, manga titles, kids comics, and science fiction stories. She's colored *Phineas and Ferb*, *SpongeBob*, *THE 99*, and *Star Wars*. Monica's favorite activities are bike riding and going to museums with her husband and two young sons. ★

about the
ARTIST

Vancey Labat got his start at Marvel Comics before moving on to illustrate children's books from *Hello Kitty* to *Peanuts* for Scholastic, as well as books for Chronicle Books, ABC Mouse, and others. His book *How Many Jellybeans?* with writer Andrea Menotti won the 2013 Cook Prize for best STEM (Science, Technology, Education, Math) picture book from Bank Street College of Education. He has two super hero girls of his own and lives in Cupertino, California. ★

about the
LETTERER

Janice Chiang has lettered *Archie*, *Barbie*, *Punisher* and many more. She was the first woman to win the Comic Buyer's Guide Fan Awards for Best Letterer (2011). She likes weight training, hiking, baking, gardening, and traveling. ★

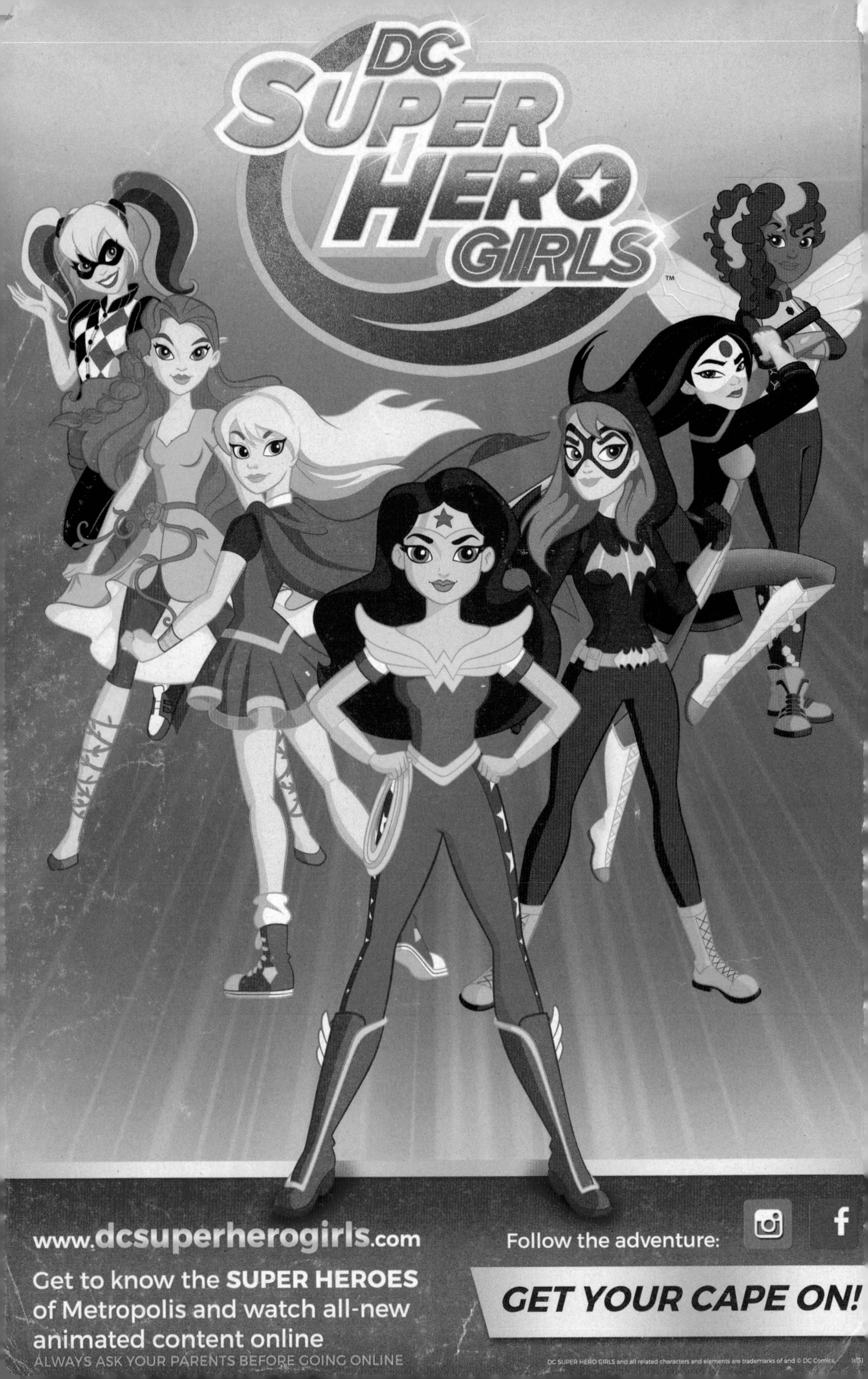

DC
SUPER HERO GIRLS
TM
www.dcsuperherogirls.com
Get to know the SUPER HEROES of Metropolis and watch all-new animated content online
ALWAYS ASK YOUR PARENTS BEFORE GOING ONLINE
Follow the adventure:
GET YOUR CAPE ON!
DC SUPER HERO GIRLS and all related characters and elements are trademarks of and © DC Comics. (s15)